# 7 WAYS TO SUNDAY

# 7 WAYS TO SUNDAY

### STORIES BY LEE KVERN

ENFIELD
&WIZENTY

Enfield & Wizenty
(An imprint of Great Plains Publications)
233 Garfield Street
Winnipeg, MB R3G 2M1
www.greatplains.mb.ca

Great Plains Publications gratefully acknowledges the financial support provided for its publishing program by the Government of Canada through the Canada Book Fund; the Canada Council for the Arts; the Province of Manitoba through the Book Publishing Tax Credit and the Book Publisher Marketing Assistance Program; and the Manitoba Arts Council.

Design & Typography by Relish New Brand Experience
Cover by Carl Wiens
Printed in Canada by Friesens

Library and Archives Canada Cataloguing in Publication

Kvern, Lee, 1957-, author
    7 ways to Sunday / Lee Kvern.

Short stories.
Issued in print and electronic formats.
ISBN 978-1-926531-85-4 (pbk.).--ISBN 978-1-926531-86-1 (epub).--
ISBN 978-1-926531-87-8 (mobi)

    I. Title.  II. Title: Seven ways to Sunday.

PS8621.V47S49 2013         C813'.6         C2013-908534-3
                                            C2013-908535-1

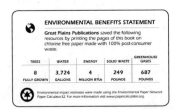

*My boys, my loves, my great big family*

# Contents

## Acknowledgements

Wild versus farmed; short story collections. Being a writer who mostly learned the craft of fiction outside the universities and colleges that have over these last two decades, awarded their hardworking, expert writers, a Masters degree, or the holy grail of a PhD, I am of the latter variety. Wild. Largely unschooled, or perhaps more accurately, randomly schooled by mentors and amazing writers who have taught me this ambiguous craft of fiction. And I certainly don't mean farmed in any derogatory sense of the word, more that I learned the liar's craft by hell and bent wheels, trials and multiple errors in good story judgment.

And here, after some twenty years of writing, is my imperfect example of that writer-in-the-wild. The stories in this collection represent my fledging years, my middle age, and recently my older, supposedly wiser (debatable) years in short story adventures. But more importantly (at least to me) this collection represents a life lived, mine and so many others that have influenced, impacted, affected me in ways that I could do nothing less than render them into story. For that, for wilds, for life, for friends, for my family, for writers from any farm, I am enormously grateful.

In no discernible order, I acknowledge:

My readers, both interior and exterior: The Lovelies, The Senior Belts, The Banff Centre, Leighton Studios, Canada Council, Alberta Foundation for the Arts, CBC National, joyland.ca, Foundpress.com, subTerrain, CBC Calgary, en-Route, Alberta Literary Awards, Event, Little Fiction, Western Magazine Awards, Hazel Hilles Memorial Prize. Mentors: first and best, Fred Stenson and Roberta Rees, Zsuzsi Gartner, Michael Helm, Curtis Gilliespie.

As well, the flood of people and readers and family that twenty years has bestowed upon me: Kelly Gray, Bobbie Charron, Dani Kvern, Jody Kvern, Erin Sisson, Nicole Ancion. Barb Howard, Betty-Jane Hegerat, Ellen Kelly, Shirley Black, Marlene Mackie. Susan Kelly, Marina Endicott, Stephen Gobby. Maureen and Blake Schulz, Lisa and Richard Price, my missed mother Barbara, my beloved father Semi, my awesome-in-laws, Beverly and Anthony Rasporich: all of whom without their literary/family/friendly help and support, I'd still be a fledging. Stephen Ives, my Arkansas phone-a-friend. Todd Babiak and Barbara Gowdy for kind words. Maurice Mierau for choosing my collection, and Gregg Shilliday for his light, trustful editing. Carl Wiens, whose art I am honoured to have on my cover. My alter ego, my supreme husband in art and life and love and crime, Paul Rasporich. My remarkable sons, Seth and Kai Rasporich, who by sheer force of fierce blood, are obliged to read their mother's work.

## White

We pull up in our Honda Odyssey, park beside the barrage of half-ton, one-ton, two-ton trucks at Lake Byrne. Not a lake found on any map but a trout-stocked irrigation pond on Byrne's back forty near Caroline; Byrne, the brother of my girlfriend's husband. We go despite the flat white on the horizon, the glittering ice crystals in the still, sunless air, the hard cold of a minus 20 day, frost clinging to the looped barbwire around the perimeter of the lake to keep the cows or the RCMP out, we don't know which, the pungent odour of pot lingering in the air as my husband unsnaps Jaxen and Chase from their car seats, the large bonfire on the edge of a mapless lake, the smash of white strangers around the fire we don't know save for my girlfriend Ella and her husband, and barely-the-brother Byrne. Nary the hint of colour beneath their skin, third-generation yellow beneath ours.

We pass a running Plymouth, the windows dressed in rime. Inside: two steamy, half-dressed teenagers ravaging one another. My husband raises a brow at me. Avert, avert, I want to say to my boys: Chase, who is two, Jaxen, four. Avert your eyes; turn away, this knowledge not yet for you. Instead I point toward the frozen lake where a group of boys are ice fishing, a crack-the-whip line of girl skaters fishtail by us, some older boys playing hockey.

"We should have brought our skates," I say, lifting Chase in my arms because the snow is two-feet deep and he's three-feet small. Jaxen in his orange fluorescent parka and Buzz

Lightyear boots stomps the ground in anticipation of ice and augers, metal hooks and cutthroat trout.

"Mind if we fish?" my husband asks Byrne, locating him in the crowd around the bonfire by the Daliesque handlebar moustache that is his signature, a cattle buyer by trade, man of few words in his off time.

"Have at 'er," Byrne says, sweeping his fleshy hand over the frozen vista. "Mind the other end."

He points to the far end of the lake: black open water, the chug chug chug of a pump. Faint trace of alcohol about him, the sharp scent of pot on Byrne's mackinaw too, and him some fifty years old.

"Busted for dealing," Ella told me years back. "He spent some time away."

"Hmm," I said, having stopped all that nonsense decades ago. "Makes you kinda thick, don't you think?"

Ella didn't reply. She still smokes pot with her husband who doesn't drink anymore because he's a recovering alcoholic. Recovering from what? I'd like to ask but don't.

Ella wanders down to the ice with us, a beer bottle hanging loosely from her left thumb. Byrne's two razor-eared Dobermans run sideways along the shore, zigzagging up and down the bank and around to the far end of the lake where the pump is—black open water.

"Stay away from there," I point, pinpointing danger's exact location. Chase pushes his cold nose into my cheek, tightens his Winnie-the-Pooh mittens around my neck. Jaxen is pulling at the canvas bag with the hand auger that my husband brought along.

"Slow going," my husband says after fifteen minutes work, his breath corporeal, a pallid cloud expanding around his head. He turns it over to Jaxen who turns turns turns the red-handled auger on the white waxy ice in his blue mittens with all his four-year-old might—the surface barely scratched.

Ella takes a long swallow, wags her empty beer bottle.

"Want one?" she asks.

My husband declines, I shake my head. She goes off in search of Byrne's gas-powered auger, another beer.

Byrne and some of the men come down from the bonfire: faces unshaven like stubble wheat, their eyes distant, dark like the open water beyond, dead-serious like Byrne, a funeral of men. Beside Byrne, a six-foot-five Goliath with a shaved head and the incongruity of Bic blue-lettered L O V E etched into the scabbed knuckles of his gloveless hands. He eyeballs us. Him I could imagine burning white crosses on his back forty in Caroline.

Goliath and the men stand as a city crew, watch Byrne position the gas-powered auger on the ice. My husband holds Jaxen back by his shoulders. Byrne pulls the cord and pushes down on the auger. At first the ice resists, bold retaliation, causes the auger to buck and rear under Byrne's sizeable weight like an edgy steer. And for one splendid moment between the awful rip of noise in the otherwise silent air, amid the burly-shouldered men of few words, between the white spray of impenetrable ice and the purple wheeze of farm gas, when it seems neither one will give way, then the frozen lake relents, groaning *uncle* as it gives in to the auger making headway, tossing shards of ice like incidental shrapnel at the lot of us.

And in the shatter of a moment, it's done: two dark-mouthed holes in Lake Byrne, one for Chase, one for Jaxen. I smile; my husband shakes Byrne's reluctant hand. Chase squirms from my arms and on hands and knees, tiny face pressed to the ice, peers down into the black holes. The men, Goliath and Byrne, retreat back to the bonfire. No words exchanged.

My husband ties J-curved hooks on strands of invisible fish line, so that when Chase and Jaxen raise their poplar branches, the metal-barbed hooks hang in the air as if suspended by magic, by mind freak, some freak of mind you couldn't otherwise imagine. On the horizon the sky is white, the white air the same temperature as the ice, the white strangers around the fire—enough to turn the rose of your flattish cheeks, the tips of your exposed fingers white white white, frostbite white.

While the boys fish, I go ashore to the bonfire, the smash of people I don't know save for Ella, her husband, barely-the-brother Byrne. She links her arm in mine, lights a cigarette. The teenage boy and girl finished ravaging one another emerge from the steamy Plymouth and stand dishevelled, replete in their open Hurley/Nikita hoodies around the blazing fire. The boy tosses in bits of wood, wrecked lawn furniture, and as the day progresses/digresses, something inappropriate like a car or one of the broken-down quads will also end up in the fire. There'll likely be a fight afterwards.

The boy's mother in the crowd is easy to pick out; she looks exactly like him except for the hailed-out look on her face. The boy rummages through her purse for a lighter but finds an aerosol can of Final Net instead. He looks at his mother before tossing it into the fire. The crowd steps back. No one says anything. The mother draws on her filterless Player's between the straight lines of her wordless lips. I glance at Ella. She's filling a red plastic cup with hot chocolate, the piquant pulse of peppermint schnapps. No words, no raised brow for her. The worlds we straddle for one another.

I go back to my husband. My yellow boys are curled around black holes, poplar sticks with line flashing visible/invisible in the murky light, gold-barbed hooks beneath the surface, danger for the trout below. Then a whoop and a holler from a boy in a black jacket, his over-large jeans cinched around his groin, grey tartan boxers, age ten at most. He's caught a cutthroat. The boy pulls it out, red and yellow-green, silver, the only colour of the day. The fish lands on the ice with a dull meaty thud, thrashes wildly until Byrne comes down and thwacks it on the head with his beer bottle: Canadian I am, he is, fish wasn't. The boy grins. The other kids squeal in mock horror, but Jaxen's shock is unfeigned.

"Better that way," my husband explains to Jaxen's sickened face. "The water their air, our air their demise."

Chase, too young or unfazed, goes over to admire the swiftly fading colours on the cutthroat along with the crack-the-whip line of girls. The teenage hockey players swoop in for a look, then blur off across the ice. Jaxen stands apart.

"Home?" I ask my husband.

"Not yet," he says.

And indeed, despite himself, Jaxen can't help but be drawn into the circle. He leans down to examine the silver-dead mercury of the cutthroat's eye.

The razor-eared Dobermans come barrelling across the lake to the circle of children. My husband blocks the black, lean-muscled animals, tries to shoo them away. The dogs stand ten feet out, watch the children, but mostly the whereabouts of the fish that the kids pass back and forth amongst themselves like a treasure, the younger ones running their bare fingertips over the slick silvery scales, awed by the red violent slash like blood beneath the cutthroat's gills.

The Dobermans tire of waiting and lope off to the other end of the lake where they wrap themselves in the fishing line of an elderly woman in a blue parka with matching hair. No doubt

Byrne's mother from the dire expression on his already-funeral face as he sprints past us, surprisingly agile for a man his size. He loses his beer bottle in the process. Byrne bellows at the dogs that immediately cease their whinging, their brutish jumping about. The dogs lie at the feet of Byrne's mother while Byrne expertly cuts the tangled fishing line from around his mother's legs with a bowie knife he produced from the shank of his left boot; the knife's end is curved up, dangerous-looking, designed to finish more efficiently.

The mother straightens up, smoothes her parka over her body. The Dobermans take off, running the quarter section that is Byrne's, and soon they are only two black dots/dogs on the white horizon. Byrne gathers his mother and on the way past us retrieves his beer bottle/fish killer, which he hands over to the ten-year-old boy in the black jacket like a rite of passage.

The kids scatter back to their respective holes. And while Chase can't see beneath the surface, he knows the fish are there from the yelps of the other children, the despondent dance of coloured fish caught in the air that is not theirs. The hockey players rip over, stopping precariously close, snowing the children in a spray of white in order to witness the number of thwacks required to make a fish say *uncle*.

Jaxen averts his gaze from the other children, fixes his eyes on the hole cut into the ice just for him, maintains the law of himself.

Chase jerks his poplar stick in and out of the hole. His eyes burn with anticipation.

"Patience," I say.

"Neath?" he asks.

I nod. He gets down on his belly to check the hole once more. After a moment he jerks his head up.

"Neath!" he yells.

A cutthroat must have swum past. He looks confused, too young yet to comprehend the dark live things that swim beneath the surface. The hockey players flash past too close, then seeing no fish, continue on.

"Watch out," I warn Chase. "Stay close."

Chase grins up at me from the ice, two tiny rows of white teeth. I nudge him gently with my Sorels across the surface like a curling rock.

Then Jaxen yelps, his face ablaze. My husband goes over and tests the line.

"Yeppers," he confirms.

Jaxen tugs the poplar stick once, twice, five times and out comes the cutthroat, its body ablaze with hoary-steaming colour. My husband removes the J hook from its mouth with a pair of needle-nose pliers; the fish falls the short distance to the ice and thrashes about. Jaxen's grin broad on his small face.

"Wait," my husband says. "We need a picture."

He looks around; we left the camera in the van.

He heads towards the shore.

The three of us stand, watch the fish hammer about on the ice. No Byrne in sight, no beer bottles, nothing but the dilemma of fish versus fate versus cruelty versus kindness. The smile on Jaxen's face ebbs and flows as the cutthroat struggles. Regardless, he and Chase dance on the surface of Lake Byrne in their small booted feet, no weight to speak of yet, barely a footprint on this immense, round earth. They take turns petting it, Chase speaking softly in his two-year-old gibberish, Jaxen laying his mittened hand on the flank of the fish as if to keep it warm, ease its suffering. Gradually the thrashing subsides, the colours fade to silver, and it looks then as if made of metal, a metal cutthroat, invincible, indestructible, can swim through the muddy heart of the underworld earth and rock and soil.

Jaxen picks up the fading fish. He's taking it back to the hole.

"Neath?" Chase asks, ruddy child-cheeks.

Jaxen looks at me, searches the shore for his father. He wants a picture but he wants even more to take the fish back. I nod. Beaming, Jaxen starts towards the cylindrical hole in the ice, the underworld below, and the fish flops in his hands, one final attempt. Jaxen loses his grip. The cutthroat drops neatly to the ice like a puck, like *Hockey Night in Canada* in slow-mo replay, perfectly timed for the show of white, the glint of steel blades, the wooden sticks of the hockey players. Up close: their teenage faces intense, pimply, a film of freezing sweat on their brows, faraway eyes already marked by life. *Fish on the ice, fair game*—the dark of their pubescent laughter. In the splinter of a second they whiz across the ice, passing the still-live cutthroat efficiently back and forth between their sticks. Jaxen in his Buzz Lightyear boots, Chase in his matching Pooh Bear hat and mittens watch as the teenagers spread out to the far side of Lake Byrne. In the distance we can see the Dobermans running towards them.

"Hey!" my husband shouts across the ice.

Chase and Jaxen look up at me: grave, funeral faces. We stand in the still sunless air of a hard, cold minus 20 day, surrounded by roiled barbwire, the flat horizon on the white prairie, the still-flat earth of white Caroline. We witness *fish/live/ puck*. Jaxen's eyes well up, Chase's too—even he understands there is no taking it back now.

I pick up Chase. My husband gathers Jaxen. We walk to the shore; find Ella in the crush of people. I lightly brush

## White

my wordless lips against her cheek; my husband declines the peppermint hot chocolate she offers. A collective cloud of smoke, pot, filterless Player's, the cold breath of white strangers hangs tangibly in the air above the fire. Someone has thrown something in the fire, not a car or a quad but a winter boot so that the smoke blackens, smells like burning soles.

## Beautiful Morning

Atticus's future girl was the one in the white sailor hat, the tight dark clothing, melancholy look about her tenuous jaw, the fragile pink around her eyes, darkened green irises the colour of the Hudson River that he found so captivating. Where, later in summer, Atticus could be found daily on the flat, wide rocks just beyond the Jewish newspaper seller for his early morning swims.

But here, this third Sunday in May, was Atticus's future girl, a quiet intense black swirl across the teeming room of the defunct, grounded ferry on Newton Creek. The makeshift bar of the ferry was covered in heavy frayed rotting rope gathered the past week from boat salvage yards, empty gasoline cans strewn about the closed-in space, the water-wracked ATM machine, discarded Bic lighters by the dozens collected from Jones/Brighton/Long Beach, from Coney Island. The rows of benches were outfitted with orange flotation devices, the yeasty waft in the stale air from the past festering carpets, thanks be only for the giddy coat of whitewash administered by Atticus and his art groupies hours prior, the oil paint still tacky on the ferry walls. On deck at midnight, a women's boxing match would take place: satin shorts, black-laced boots, red leather gloves, no sucker punches, K.T.F.O. (knocked the fuck out), semi-professionals only.

# Beautiful Morning

The girl, like the rest of his followers, made it out to the derelict ferry turned performance art turned party boat; the third annual *Nautical Waste* Atticus staged with fellow artists, urban outlaws, and/or any other stray act-full New Yorkers interested in art, or simply the spirit of drunken, mutinous sailors.

The sailor girl fit neatly, categorically into both art and mutinous, a scrimshaw artist of some small note he would find out later, her skilled lewd, erotica scenes of couples engaged in, with, joined to one another, etched rousingly, mostly on old piano keys, (mammoth tusks and walrus ivory hard to come by these days, endangered like scrimshaw itself) like her, also, Atticus suspected. The lovely blue veins that pulsed beneath her brown skin, wound along her delicate wrists, the sheer hollow of her temples, the small glass of uncut vodka she held in her precise hands.

Atticus's eyes laid exactly on her, her eyes cast on the live-black merman standing in the corner next to the giant penis Atticus constructed from the million plastic bags and sea-sanitized condoms washed ashore, tied and stuffed, swollen beyond recognition, spray painted blue to match the black merman. His girl as mesmerized as Atticus by the live merman's African-American body embodied from the waist down in fish-tailed bubble wrap, a skiff of fluorescent blue riffing off the surface of his skin as if newly enlightened, fairy dust of some kind, fairly glistening off his defined pectorals, over the silver-pierced nipples, across his muscle cut abdomen.

Atticus watched his girl manoeuvre through the swim of young/old men and women: mostly single, creative solitary souls—their world of constant dread. Though few were married, still filled with hope, working multiple jobs, this city so expensive they could hardly find a place to lay their own hard-treading artistic heads down, let alone hope for children and a reasonable life beyond. So many had left. So many had given up, in, over. Others filled with the street, illicit substances, homeless, hopeless, the mottled mix of artists/dancers/writers/poets/performance artist packed in the room like discounted fish in a metal can. The blue-black of his girl's short cropped hair shimmered beneath the pot lights as if freshly created, matching the otherworld hue of the merman's skin, a glistening blue—the both of them meticulous performances on their own, some glorious nautical specimens Atticus fished out of the tidal depths of the lower Hudson.

♦

Future girl: Long before Pali knew him, she knew him, his public him. His loves: giant squid, his metal cat series that he rarely, occasionally sold, his beloved mother, her generous trust fund, his *Sell Hell* mosaic constructed secretly, publicly beneath the Brooklyn Bridge, his home-built fiberglass and wood submarine that he launched in the Hudson River in honour of the Revolutionary War that earned him two Coast Guard citations and the front page of the *New York Times*. (No real terrorist threat, the *Times* reported, just marine mischief.) His urban outlaw-ness that propelled him to seek the forgotten parts of the city, the vacant space where water met land, or in the middle of waters, those rarefied places not yet claimed by land developers; his obsession with the lower Hudson, perhaps its free connection to the open sea, or the marrying of foreign waters. Pali didn't know which or why. The beard he longed for but couldn't grow, the nautical braided hair, the graffito wire fish he constructed, embedded into the rusty hulls of deserted vessels around the harbours.

His flat work pinned, stapled, taped to billboards, fence posts, construction sites: giant mono-toned etchings of squids, pen and ink drawings of strangely joined marine creatures, sharp finned, sparking red lightning out of their tails, mouths open, laughing, eyes shut. His moniker, the two-starred flag, Liberty or Death that he spray painted on walls throughout the Meatpacking District, his art not for sale, never for owner-ship—only, always for public consumption. The steel sculpted spike-backed cats welded (with permission by the liberal parish priest who also ran a program for the homeless) on the stone steps of the rear entrance of Our Lady of Guadalupe on West 14th where Atticus was living temporarily in the lower bowels: a windowless, one-roomed spacious bunker.

Pali knew the litany/legend of his body art, the skipping, stippling tattoos, so naughty, nautical, scrimshaw-like, elaborate drawings on a minuet scale displayed across the cagey surface of his salted skin, first in Pali's mind as she watched him across the crowded room behind the makeshift bar. Then later with Pali's soft mouth and renewed hands, every lucent pore of her Spanish body finding them, discovering him bit by bit like bits of startling treasure washed up on shore or tiny illuminated glints half buried in the sand, beneath his clothes. The double-ended eel snaking the electric line of wiry brown hair down his lower belly, the curled, almost hidden birds, fish, flowers, coloured songs rippling beneath the muscle of his shoulder blades, his chest, all of it—him registering beyond the rigid moral constructs of land, life, her mother. In Atticus, a sense of danger and possibility. How could Pali not? Seventeen years junior to his forty, an only child to her strict Catholic mother, deadbeat father (oh father where art thou?). Only hers to decide. Pali crossed the room to claim him.

"Pali Caliente," she said extending her small hand directly into his.

▲

The day she moves into his life, Atticus fleshes out a corner for her in the roomy church bunker, a rickety kitchen table he found on Washington Street that he reinforced with metal brackets beneath each wobbly leg.

"For you," he showed Pali, "and us."

Unpacking a bag of still-hot cinnamon buns from the Portuguese bakery two doors down, thanks to monthly stipends from his lovely mother in Upper Manhattan. From behind his back he produces two peeled mangoes on pointed sticks from the Jamaican street vendor above, like a bouquet of flowers, deep yellow, the undertone of Pali's golden skin in July, the faint blue/red of her perceptible veins that make him lie awake at night sometimes and ache, those haunting Hudson River eyes. But the mango fruit in season, dripping oh so sweet sticky down their moving, searching mouths, so smooth sure faces while Atticus produces strong black Americanos on his Italian Krups each morning. Overhead the bright silver swinging light for their late morning brunches that sometimes bled into lunch, their leisurely dinners: life-taking, art-making, love-finding all found on a tenuous table in the basement of a Roman Catholic church.

🌑

Pali's slight shoulders hunched in the corner, her blackened clothing, her etching tools strict, disciplined like her mother but different, she imagines, hers chosen, created, not the forced religious-rote life that her mother blindly followed. Pali's honed knives, large-eyed needles, sharpened scribes that she scratches, stipples on the difficult surface of lost lives, ancient bones, found ivories. Tiny, intricate holes fortified with the soothing voices of her pale-coloured pigments filling in the prescribed spaces of human body upon body in the controlled, confined space of piano keys, the odd whalebone when available; her couples coupled, pleasure-seeking, the effervescent sensual music of them, her art, her vibrant Atticus blocking out the sound of her otherwise hissing sibilant life.

"Come look," she'd say and Atticus would lay down his black Sharpie, cross the wide room, his calloused hands needing the tight ball of her hunched shoulders.

"Us," she'd tell him.

"Listen."

The soft hush of the forced air, the muted footfall of Sunday mass above; the blank look on Atticus's face, nonetheless his wide chipped-toothed smile, his needy massage that distracts her brilliantly from her intense work.

🌑

And Atticus a veritable feast, a never-die light, a seemingly giant squid himself, multi-armed with graffiti cans of spray paint, his tubes of bright acrylics, an art happening wherever he happened to be. His studio visitors: friends, followers, the liberal priest from above checking from time to time to make sure nothing ungodly was taking place below his feet, beneath his church. Pali sliding her piano keys beneath the soft cotton cloth she used to clean her tools. The odd time Atticus's mother in full swing, full-length fur/cashmere/chiffon coat, cherry lipped and smiling tightly at the mere acquaintances, the off-the-street bearded, pierced, shaved, mohawked, land-locked strangers that Atticus equips with plastic ice cream pails filled with shattered ceramics, broken tea cups and tiles, bits of sea glass.

"Look, look what I found!" Atticus waving his finds in the air for Pali to see.

Beer glass, found on-the-street glass, the accompanying buckets of Thinset mortar and metal trowels; him and his followers spread out across the city like seabirds, foraging the hidden places, the darkened bits of the city, the vacant spots in need of light. A spray/acrylic/mosaic minstrel, Atticus leads his followers up and down the streets of his great city, the world's eye solely on his apple.

"Want to come?" he asks Pali.

Pali looks up, a conflicted longing in her Hudson eyes, she shakes her head; leans closer to the whalebone she's inking melancholy blue in the lightless room.

"See you after?" he asks.

She looks across the room, flashes her small ivory teeth at him.

"Of course."

♟

Summer days Pali works well into the night. The windowless room in the church basement discerning neither the light nor the dark, the muffled footsteps of the parish priest above her head, the whispery confessions she thinks she can hear, the classical: forgive me father I've sinned, or bless me father for I kicked me wife's cat this morning, Irish Catholic that one. She doesn't really know, mostly makes up the imagined dialogue in the stony silence, the inky smudge of quiet voices, distant music in her light-depraved brain; too long alone.

It doesn't matter now the hours bent over the hard wood surface, the pointed tools, porous ivory, her pulsating Atticus more and more absent. She wanders the dark room in her dark clothing, where is Atticus? Out with friends, followers, creating organized disorder on the streets of New York for the people of New York. She gets it; she really does, his public self, his private driven need to be unrestricted, freely available, publicly known, his enviable freedom that she sometimes envies.

But she's lonely tonight, tired, she wants him here, his lean lush body curled around hers on their stripped futon on the cement floor, the tender of his skin, the song of his tattoos, not the relentless murmur in her head that she can't drown out.

She goes down the quiet hall to the bathroom, fishes through the medicine cabinet, finds the muscle relaxants Atticus had when he threw his back out trying to haul a large metal grate out of the Hudson, perfect for the temporary bar instal-lation he was planning for Plum Island: the reconstructed shanty town turned street chic, concrete building to be freshly graffiti-ed, salvaged sea bottles to be washed and cleaned, filled with booze, five-cent crabs steamed, served at midnight, all compliments of his mother's trust fund, if only she knew. Atticus's goal: make it until morning, then pass out in the sea air, nothing better.

He'd dragged the heavy, river-rusted grate along the banks of the estuary, then back along West Street until finally he sat down on the curb, heavy breathing, clutching his lower back, he abandoned it out of sheer exhaustion. Like her perhaps, her exhaustion, his abandonment? She opens the childproof prescription bottle with both hands, such force the small bottle slips out of her hands, the tiny blue pills dispersing on the concrete floor. She bends down, pops two in her mouth, doesn't bother to gather the rest, she'll find them later. She downs the pills with a shot of uncut vodka, then pours herself another shot, nothing serious, no intent. Settles on their futon for a long Atticus-less night.

♟

So maybe she goes looking for him the places she knows, they places they go together: Flatiron, West Village, not necessarily NoHo or Greenwich but along 11th Ave behind the closed Jewish newspaper stand, the stand of flat rocks overlooking the Hudson River. The moon high, full bright, the New York air hot, humid still. She feels so good, a flotation device, more buoyant than she has her entire life. The pills yes, the vodka shots, the saline thick in the moist air like Atticus's skin when he comes home after his early morning swims. She thinks of Atticus's wiry body moving through the green morning water.

"Beautiful morning?" The Jewish newspaper seller apparently asks Atticus after each of his morning swims.

No doubt her Atticus nodding vigorously, standing on the wide rocks, rivulets of Hudson streaming off his coloured fish, his flowers, his roaring birds, his beautiful stripped-down body.

# Beautiful Morning

"Beautiful morning," Atticus bellowed whenever he came home, a paper bag in hand.

Her blue-black hair a tumble, she rising, yawning from the futon, the yellow sun through the opened door.

"What did you bring?"

The broad grin across his beardless face, forty years old, no handles on his waist you could call love, nothing to hang onto but she does anyway. So strong his strokes, so certain his swimmers touch, their simple physical exchange. After: Ukrainian poppy bread or jam kolaches or sugar-dusted Polish chruscik, Italian panettone—their world of constant bread.

In the humid night, she pulls her knees up on the flat, still-warm rocks, squints out over the quiet water. She wants to feel him now, feel his electric eel body coupled, conjoined with hers. She doesn't want his public commodity anymore. She wants him. She takes her Blancpain watch (Moon series), such an extravagant gift from Atticus's mother (seriously an apartment would make more sense but Atticus refuses anything beyond his mother's monthly stipends on which he funds his installations and subsists in the cement bunker of an 18th century church). This watch, this gift a sure sign that Pali might well be the one able to withstand both eccentric mother and give-me-liberty-or-find-me-death son. Pali strips her layers of tight black clothing off down to her lemon-coloured bra and cotton boy briefs, folds them neatly into a pile on the flat rock, lays the Blancpain watch on top; a small dip to cool her ravenous skin, the compelling moon glinting off the surface of the deep green Hudson.

First light, his followers dispersed back to home, alleyways, park benches, river shores, Atticus alone descends the stone stairs into the cement bowels of the church. Catches the flesh of his right ankle on the spiked cat in the murky light. Reaches down, wipes the blood away but it keeps coming, deeper than he thought, so that he must pause, the stinging pain reverberating up his calf. He sits on the bottom step in the uncertain dawn, removes his sock and ties it around the gash, applies sufficient pressure until his blood coagulates, thickens and the throbbing pulse lessens. He pushes the heavy wood door open, waits for his eyes to adjust to the black, limps quietly down the hall, and opens the door to their stone bunker.

"Beautiful morning," he bellows.

No answer. He squints into the room: the sun revealing his marine mono-prints taped on the walls. Pali's reinforced wood table in the corner, the silver lamp she's left on for him. He glances at their bed for his Pali Caliente unclothed, the smooth brown Spanish skin, her beautiful slight body sprawled naked across the length of their bare futon. She's not there. He walks over, grimacing at the immediate memory of his ankle, the deep flesh wound (he might require stitches), peers closely at the assembly line of piano keys, her latest scrimshaw project, a series of swimming fish, roaring birds, human figures rolling, conjoined, intertwined both above and seemingly below the porous surface of the ivory as if three dimensional, Pali's sleight of hand he thinks, or is it the watery pale of her coloured inks, like tattooed bones? It lulls him suddenly, sharply into the idea of ownership. He doesn't mind so much. He runs his fingers across the keys, imagines he hears the faint, distant music.

Us, he thinks.

He goes down the dark hall, knocks tentatively on the bathroom door. No answer there either. Restless perhaps, too long at work, Pali gone to the Cuban market on 8th for guava rolls, her favourite. Not unusual. He goes into the bathroom, slaps cold water on his tired, otherwise slaphappy face, only the medicine cabinet, the empty bottle of muscle relaxants cause him to swallow the first gallows of his future sorrow.

♟

She doesn't mean it, never would, but it happens anyway. The circulation in her arms going first in the undertow, the wild Hudson so certain, so physical, so powerful, such risk she couldn't have guessed, the merciless cold that surprises her. Then her legs won't move, she can't lift her head, can no longer see the moon's extraordinary light skipping across the surface, instead her body dipping, slipping down. The still-dancing light above her head now, the tidal waters holding her, a weird, cruel buoyancy just below the surface, unrelenting but kindly almost as if she could reach up and wave, feel the New York air warm and gorgeous on her porous skin. Strangely she can't or doesn't want to. It doesn't seem to matter.

Listening to the nothing she hears under the water, the paradoxical calm once her thrashing subsides. Certainly not what she expected, so deceptively strong, so sure in its grip, its touch, her apparent lack of stroke. Mere feet below the surface of the lower Hudson, the necessary circuit in her body running from groin to heart, then her organs one-by-one, bit by bit, the cold telling her heart to stop, beat, love. There is nothing she can do.

▲

As surely as if he'd found the pile of neatly folded black clothing, Pali's Blancpain watch laid out on the flat rocks, which he
didn't, (instead a blue bin diver from East Village lucked out).
Nonetheless Atticus knows. He takes his threadbare white tee
off, lays his Armani flip-flops aside that he found on Bank Street
the previous week, mere days before the series of lightless days/
nights in the church basement, a subterranean vault, the liberal
priest, his beloved mother, his followers checking-in on an
hourly basis until finally he triple-bolted the door from the
inside and refused to respond. Of the unbearable waiting
no sleep no Pali no relief. He unbuttons his ripped jeans, no
boxers beneath, only the double-ended eel of his silent tattoo
snaking down his flat belly to his pubis to the mortal coil of
his penis.

A strong swimmer, familiar with the heavy undertow of the
Hudson, where to swim, where not to, he wades in—the spiky
sting of salt on his cut ankle. He forgot his watch; not water-
proof, no gratuitous gift from his mother, his watch purchased
cheap from a Lebanese street vendor, Obama's optimistic face,
the screaming red, white and blue of America flagging the background, two hands circling as if waving. He wades out of the
estuary, lays the novelty watch on his faded white tee. The
evening sun glinting off the river's surface, eager for his naked
body, eager for his desperate pumping blood, the complicated
neurons of his bright mind, the bright of Pali's mistaken day;
he knows where she is.

He dives down, reaches under for as long as he can, his
lungs screaming beneath the Hudson as he slips through the
dark green water, the searing pain a temporary balm on his

permeable skin, then he surfaces. Choking, sobbing, saline flooding his mouth, his eyes, he splutters, gasps, not trying for breath but the opposite. His hands circling, survival instinct, the buoyant water, not the pitch black, the sink, the fall, the drop, the permanent descent below the dazzling surface of the Hudson, the K.T.F.O. he wants so badly; coupled with his Pali in the sea of mud, the subterranean basement of a living river.

Instead the steady, maniac autonomy of his forty years, his wiry arms, his wary body, muscular legs matching his front crawl. Beneath the coloured fish, the flowers, the scrimshaw-like birds on his chest the bastard beat beat beat of his heart that won't stop, the involuntary in/out/in/out of his breath that he can't control—harder than he thought, not what he expected, not the nothingness he intended. So strong his strokes, so certain his intent, this seemingly simple physical exchange between man and water, above/below the permeable surface of the Hudson.

Further than he's been in the channel, tidal waves slapping up against his face, he pauses, grief's roar in his ears, his frantic breath, he can't make out her music, nor can he seem to make it up. The throbbing in his head, his chest, his hidden places, his darkened bits, his vacant spot in need of light, he treads water, watches the sun wane, lose its fullness, the warmth leaching as it drops on the Hudson horizon. The darkness settles around him in the channel. Still he swims, if he can make it through the night—then his fierce, beautiful mourning.

♟

In the lemon light of dawn, the Jewish newspaper seller rolls back the metal gates, stacks the weekend-thick *New York*

*Times,* displays the daily papers, rearranges the glossy maga-
zines, spots the pile of clothing on the flat rocks. Shielding his
eyes from the brightness, he walks over, gathers the clothing,
straps the Obama watch on his left wrist, for later, for safe-
keeping, squints out over the green Hudson for the swimmer,
no doubt the wiry man he sees each morning.

# Fourteen

The boy is fourteen, old enough to work but not necessarily old enough to man the seafood counter at Sobeys. A slack-bellied, receding-haired man in sweat pants stands in front of the boy. The boy wears black pants with a proper waistband, has shoulder-length blond hair. They are separated only by the glass tank, aerated water and forty-odd years. In the man's hand basket is a bottle of wine, a single-serve Caesar salad, garlic bread wrapped in tin foil.

The boy extracts the glistening brown lobster with two fingers and sets it on the weigh scale. The lobster's armoured body is a fair size; precisely what the customers pay fourteen dollars a pound for. It rears up like King Kong, challenging the boy with claws rendered helpless by ordinary rubber bands. The boy picks up the lobster with his thumb and forefinger. The lobster swivels his claws from side to side, and the boy almost drops it on the floor, but regains himself when he notices the man watching him. The boy tries to press the lobster into the takeout box. Lobster wins by a tail.

A woman goes by with a full-to-the-brim shopping cart, babies and straggling toddlers. The man watches her swivel down the aisle, her heart no doubt the size of her generous hips. He sees love, ample love, hips and children and all. When he looks back to see what progress the boy is making, the look in his eyes no longer applies to mere lobster longing.

The lobster is a Friday night ritual he initiated ever since his psychologist told him that one *must* fish in the sea of love in order to find love. He never understood what that meant.

"You're worth it," the psychologist enthused, like he was about to dye what little hair he had left, a L'Oréal Number 6 Red. The sweat pants don't help either, exaggerating his girth while shortening his height. His clothes, like his hair, his hope, mostly diminished.

He watches the boy struggle to put the lobster into the too-small box. The boy folds the tail down while forcing the lobster's fettered claws into the box. When the boy manages to do both at the same time, the lobster rears up from inside the box, its antennae poking out, waving around one last time before fate and cardboard close in. Both man and boy appreciate this last stand for different reasons: the boy admires its feistiness, the man, its struggle—however futile.

But it's the care with which the boy pushes the lobster down that belies the boy's innocence. The man smiles, knows full well what will happen once he gets the lobster home. The boy is young, the man thinks, has unfettered dreams, entire seas yet to come and possibly go.

Perhaps, the boy thinks, the man will take it home and name it Ronnie or Roxanne, run cool, clear water in his bathtub, take the ordinary rubber bands off the lobster's claws and let it live. Perhaps this story isn't over.

The man picks up the box and checks the price.

"A fourteen-dollar bargain," he says.

The boy presses his full, pink lips together, doesn't say anything. He's still got hope.

## High Ground

Basketball is cheaper than crack, says the coach to us parents and our teenaged children sprawled out in collapsible metal chairs in the high school cafeteria. Wisecrack grins on some of our sons' faces, but no, the coach is serious. We parents roll our eyes at each other, me, the lone, single mother in the crowd, only too familiar with the skyrocketing cost of sport. Varsity basketball costs a pretty gold Krugerrand, a precious copper these days. The coach disperses the photocopies: fees, schedules, parental expectations, player obligations to us sport-spent parents.

Questions? asks the coach. We shake our heads, fold our metal chairs, exit the high school cafeteria, our adolescent boys ahead in a noisy scrum, blood-pumping thoroughbreds primed for the season.

♟

June 19, 2013. Venue: the condemned warehouse east of downtown, no railway tracks to cross, no telltale boundaries that I can distinguish, just the flipside of a city built on cattle and a flood plain. I sit in the Camry Wagon that I bought baby-spanking new decades ago, the 4-door model in a cherry-stained colour they no longer make.

I bought it when I still had the theological concept for family: six children, steady income, stable husband. Instead the warm/soft/crazy flood of years, a brief, childless marriage, a series of potential (failed) partners. Then at age 38, a late conception, relative to the passing thought that my life might be passing me by; present single mother, Church of the Latter Day Saints, mid-menopause. Mother's note: the last father stand-in, a former Stampede linebacker, didn't make the latter meanopause (his term). He left in a freak snowstorm on May 6th two years ago.

Single again, age 55, I am old enough for early senior's discount at Rexall Drugs where I work, driving solo in a family wagon, my hair matches the gray duct tape that holds the gray plastic moulding in place on the rear window. The wheel wells of my car are blistering down to the tarnished metal beneath.

Bright spot: one son, LITTLETON, 6' 4", U-17, slam dunker, former honours with distinction. No grasping where I went wrong.

♟

I look sidelong at the abandoned warehouse that overlooks the Bow River, normally a beautiful, moving, multi-layered woozy blue this time of year, but with the late spring runoff from the crystalline Rockies and the unyielding rain for the past two weeks, the slate-coloured river is suddenly deep and violent, a seemingly mile-wide riptide. Its turbid waters riding high and fast, threatening to overtake its sandstone banks and run roughshod among the still-standing poplar trees along the boulevard.

I sip my rummed Double Double, my private *rumble* that gets me moving and beautiful in the morning. I watch the voiceless raging river, a disaster movie on mute that I can't quite connect to, no radio on in the car, no sound from the warehouse. I hold my breath.

## High Ground

The shattered window: the boy that freed up the S.E. warehouse for daytime use eviscerated himself while crawling through, at which point the unnerved crowd had no choice but to call the police in, the boy's life and freed viscera at stake. This, I heard from some of the other parents that also gather here, usually Friday or Saturday late in the dust/dusk before things heat up inside, and the sky outside grows dark—and then it's neither safe nor advisable to be in the area, present children present or not.

I sooth my hands over my slack belly, make sure my intestines are in place, think I spot the straw-straight blond hair of my son LITTLETON through the shattered window amongst the dark mix of the teens inside.

Mostly U-17's, local players, the odd child, I catch myself calling them that—their child-thin shoulders, straining ribs, my son's Jesus-skinny cheeks that I long to cup in my mother hands, if only to warm/warn them. The *children* floating across the country like some rogue weather system, unanchored, unlashed, feckless from the New Found Lands or Canada's bleating heart Toronto or the bi-linguals from Montreal, and the western biggies from beautiful British Columbia, who only come in the summer months for the Stampede parade and parties.

I know them all by sight, some by name, the sheer numbered days of my Camry surveillance. Lili, the solitary girl won't be sixteen until the following year, which no one seems to notice or care about, outside the girl's father, who comes in police clothes in his civilian car. The police officer father comes for Lili, if only for a short time to detox in order to give her minor body a break from the A-stroll; A because she's still young, still radiant, under-aged. He glances across the street at me in my worn-out Camry; faces sombre, we shake our parental heads at one another.

The urgency of his gait as he escorts his strawberry-haired daughter out of the warehouse, his brawny arm about Lili's scrawny shoulders, the unnatural sheen of her large green eyes on her emaciated face strikes me may be even more heart demolishing than my own, only son—if that's possible. I search deep inside myself, my Church of the Latter Day Saints, find instead in the rearview mirror, the cheerless grey duct tape, the raging grey river.

Despite the grainy, rainy day, the soundless roaring river, I squint through the glassless window of the warehouse, see the blue tinge of LITTLETON's shoulder-to-cuff tattoo. He's easy to identify now, no longer lost in the moving, charging, sweaty scrum of his Varsity basketball friends, their long-limbed teenage bodies like thoroughbreds in the prime of their lives, never to be again. For LITTLETON since the no-good, down-low Osgood-Schlatter disease that arrived like a bad guest last year, a host of the poorest kind, the inflammation pulling at my son's knees, rendering him in pain. Our hearts sore; LITTLETON'S and mine, our shattered hopes for his senior high year.

I watch him through the broken window. If anything, my high-driving, court-hammering LITTLETON is persistent, unyielding. He's acquired a new tattoo every month for this last sport-less year as if to mark something: a new love, a talisman of some kind, perhaps the end or the beginning?

He doesn't tell, I can't decide.

I take a slug of my rumble, the tributary of coffee and rum trickle down my chin that I wipe off with a used tissue from the dashboard. The menopausal dew breaks out across my cheeks, and suddenly, weirdly I miss that moist, musty assault of my son's rock-solid body dashing in and out of our Kensington apartment, his flock of like-smelling, basketball friends in tow, going here, there, never really sure but safely installed in some gym or food court. I miss his bare arms poking out of his Varsity jersey, the muscled, fleeting illusion of youth and hope that seem a distant memory.

And yet here, now—this is what I hold out for. I want to go back to the clean unmarked skin of his boyish arms rather than the tainted ticker tape of his blue tattoos telling the world—here is who he is now.

I can barely stand the thought.

♟

The warehouse players check in with the older boy at the door in the neon purple tracksuit, tear-away pants, and bare feet. I don't know why, but I do know the older boy, like my son, lives at home with his mother. Is he the event planner? No, more likely, he's the token team manager earning minimum wage for his water boy work. He's the first to get heated up by the police, the first to get jacked by his clients, and the courts are particularly tough on dealers, even for the first offence. It's a deadly drug game for a deadly drug dealer, who sticks around only long enough to sell his crack/rock collection.

I see my son but still I don't move.

I never do, not until he comes out, sometimes in full sunlight, the bright of those days (unlike this grey one) matching the yellow of his eyes, his muscles a tremor, limbs a twitch like Cerebral Palsy; I can only imagine what his Cerebral Cortex is doing. LITTLETON'S long legs traversing the fractured sidewalk, like he's not part of *this* world—his, mine or otherwise. As if he's on a trip to Mars, his watery eyes spotting me across the street in my cherry Camry—yet he's compelled, also, to search for the older boy in the purple tracksuit, this new love flooding his grief-stricken face, both him and me defenseless, knowing the eventual tweaking rises like a river that no one can control.

He doesn't wave. Never does.

♣

Better, latter days, October 2012. Venue: Crescent Heights. Varsity Basketball. Giddy with the smell of fresh varnish on the old gymnasium floor, the early morning mix of spectators, us parents, siblings. For the most part original sins: Adam and Eve, Barbie and Ken, the shiny mothers and fathers, our shimmering adolescent boys oblivious to the heady smell of chemical. The glossy hardwood beneath their *Air Jordans*, their *All Stars*, their *And1s* as they bounce their orange leather balls. Some younger siblings run, shriek breathlessly beneath the wood bleachers. Amid the Grande Macchiatos, the Chai Lattes, my Double Double, (no rum rumble yet, that comes later), nothing except for the buzz of bright chatter from all of us, our hopes high.

The warm-up gangsta beats are booming over the loud-speakers, almost laughable to me, hardly a menacing face on this white Wonderbread team, our clean-cut players acting out a dangerous role, the glittery surface of a shallow river, no real depth to speak of yet. But the beats are multi-layered and rhythmic, heating up the players, competing for our parental hearts, affecting us all with its deep primal bass.

The players' names emblazoned in capital letters across their *youngsta* backs, announcing to the world: MASON, THURBER, SORENSON, HUFF, LITTLETON. The team running drills, practising screens, draining/raining threes, throwing up bank shots, hook shots, finger rolls. The black and white striped referee blows his shrill whistle; our adolescent boys a-twitch with excitement, can hardly pull themselves off the wood floor, can hardly sit still long enough on the pine bench for the coach's last minute instructions, so desperate are they for the game to begin.

My son on the starting line-up: the jump off, the crisp passing, his left-handed lay ups, beauty jump shots as if choreographed, field goals, efficient screens, those fancy finger rolls, reliable lay ups. Ooh a flagrant foul, the riptide of muddy rage across LITTLETON's face, the flipside I never want to glimpse. Ride it out, I breath for him in the high wood bleachers, ride, ride, ride.

He swishes both free throws, a wisecrack grin on his face at the flagrant Crescent fouler. A minor pushing/shoving/match broken up by three shrill tweets of the ref's whistle that rings in my ears long after the fact—a stern talking to my son by the coach as if that's all it takes.

First quarter, second, the time clock rolls the game out, forever suspended in happy time, (I wish) delirious in these last few months spent in sweaty gymnasiums up and down the province, surrounded by other keen, like-minded parents and their children. If only to dispel my loneliness, if only to keep the muddy rage from flooding my son's susceptible face entirely.

All of us: yelling, clapping, booing, hissing, chanting, raining hopeful fingers for the foul shots, listing to one side or the other in the stands to catch the fast breaks, missed passes, made passes, breath-holding threes, HUFF's alley-oop in the third quarter.

The fourth quarter, my favourite, LITTLETON's fast break down the court, the grand slam a la dunk that makes our

Starbucks/Hortons crowd come up off the bleachers and roar in unison like we'd done it ourselves.

A tie game, the last twenty-six seconds stretched like silicone by both coaches: time outs, no fouls (!) the last pick and roll, possession, the outstanding rebound by Crescent, the screen, the steal by LITTLETON the defender, our players riding the gym floor high and fast and rough beneath the boards. LITTLETON's hallowed three pointer in the last eight seconds tick tick ticking down the clock, answered by a three from Crescent—this game could go either way.

We parents are sick in the stands: worry, joy, overwrought, elated, devastated, then sick again until the buzzer signals the end, the grinding rasp of time drowned out by the incredulous roar of a narrow victory, this perilous game.

♟

June 20, 2013. Venue: Same condemned warehouse.

And now they come in full uniform, not the normal blue but the serious black of the SWAT team. The river threatening to crest its sandstone banks, the slate-coloured water ready to run bedlam in our streets. But it doesn't. Not yet, not until tomorrow evening when the street here is vacant, emptied of all its players; instead the sheer respite of the pounding rain.

I know then this is no warm-up, no simple heating up: the usual checking of I.D.'s, running license plates from the cars coming and going at all hours, making it uncomfortable for the occupants inside the abandoned warehouse—on the off chance that the young players will disperse to other locations, drift back home perhaps, or across the country from whence they came. Not this time, this particular warehouse a precinct priority, the SWAT team means business.

As difficult as it is to pick out the police officer father in the sudden soundless swarm of black-clad officers, the hammering rain, I recognize the father by his height, the urgency of his gait. He's also the one with the straining-at-the-leather-leash German shepherd. He glances across the street at me in my Camry, and mouths: Lock your door.

I do.

The German shepherd is also desperate, pulling, barking, leaping wildly on the sidewalk, snarling in readiness, can hardly wait for the remaining windows of the warehouse to be smashed, the metal doors bashed down, the surprise combined entry of the SWAT team.

The police officer father gives three sharp bursts from his ceramic whistle, signalling both the SWAT team and the players inside that ready or not, the dog is coming forth. I feel the whistle more than actually hear it from inside my car, a Helen Keller vibration that resonates beneath my skin. Perversely pleasant as in LITTLETON'S better, latter days—an almost submissive relief comes over me that someone can do in the present what I cannot.

Then the warehouse is seething: live with New Found Land, displaced Ontario, bi-lingual Montreal, beautiful British Columbia, the local players rushing the freed windows, streaming out the front, the back, the side doors, up to the tarnished patina of the copper roof, triple-jumping the 10'8" gap to the abandoned office building next door. The SWAT team a coordinated effort, the swift black of uniformed officers, the boy in the neon purple tracksuit sprinting barefoot down the street, each stride the German shepherd closes the distance between them.

The whoops, the hollers, the shrillness of the whistle calling the dog off, not soon enough for the boy with the tearaway track pants rolling in the middle of the ruptured concrete shrieking breathlessly; the torrential rain. No soundtrack, no gangsta beats for this game, I watch in grateful horror.

I see my son exit the building through the shattered window. The pounding rain soaks him instantly, makes his Nash tee-shirt cling to his body all protruding ribs and sharp collarbone, the shadow of faint muscle beneath his arm slickered with blue tattoo.

As if the choreographed chaos swirling about him, the baited, rising river, the not-for-long standing poplar trees along the boulevard have nothing whatsoever to do with him or me—this indefensible world, my son walks across the street in the seizing rain. Pre-flood.

I unlock the door, LITTLETON folds his 6'4" defender frame into my ailing car, doesn't bother to lie down out of sight, sits alive and twitching in the backseat. I search my son's face in the rearview mirror, his skin the colour of muddy water, the aberrant sheen in his river eyes. My slim glimmer of hope.

Across the street the police officer father scores a hallowed three: his daughter Lili secure in the front seat, the German shepherd and neon-wet drug dealer in the back. The temporary reign of the SWAT team as they load up the sodden, sullen warehouse occupants into the large dark van. The street is empty, save for the grey, murky, swirling rising water that runs freely, rushing the fractured concrete, seeping, climbing through the broken windows of the now vacant warehouse.

The soaked-to-the-skin police officer spots my son in the backseat of my Camry. I roll down my window.

High ground, says the police officer.

## This Is A Love Crime

He covers the length of Renata's freckled body, from her Wham Bam Glam toe-nail polish up along her velvet-shaved thighs, lingering always too long at her groin, shaved and hairless like he likes it. In contrast to Corbin's hairy body that at times Renata finds repulsive. Then up her childless abdomen to her small breasts, her warm neck, her worried, moist armpits, behind her ears, her glossy black hair that hangs loose and thick down to her shoulders the way he prefers.

Renata lies perfectly still, not submissive necessarily, though her body is stiff and erect while her husband Corbin performs his animalistic ritual in confirming that she is his, his alone, his only. Luckily she's had a few drinks, easier to submit then to mutiny and spend their swiftly-passing weekends quarrelling with one another, interlocking his and her horns. She saves the weight of her humility for the other five days of the week.

No scent this Friday night beyond Joey Tomatoes, deep-fried calamari, a couple after work Crantinis with her colleagues from Save-on-Foods where Renata's worked her way up to Human Resources from her many years as Human Cashier; the reek of Phil perhaps, the Aldergrove store manager's florid, effeminate cologne; no one that Corbin need be concerned with. The residual odour of nicotine, the cigarettes she isn't to be smoking but can't, not. Not a trace of sea or strange men as Corbin sniffs her genitals like a dog—though it's Renata who feels canine.

"Are you smoking again?" he asks, resurfacing.

"No, it's the girls."

He looks at her. She looks away.

"Whose god-awful perfume?"

"Phil's," Renata says, pulling the duvet up over her exposed body cold now in the late night.

"He could at least smell like a man," Corbin says, his conversational opener that Renata doesn't respond to. Yes, Phil's gay, so what? What business is it of theirs?

"I'll inform him of that on Monday," Renata says, dryly.

Corbin breathes in the dark, not saying what she knows he's thinking. *Talk to me, for God's sake, Renata. I don't see you all week, I miss you like hell, and you can't come home and talk to me?* She knows it like the etched frown on his idealistic face. She doesn't talk.

"You can be such an asshole," he says in her silence.

She rolls over. Corbin sighs.

"Going to sleep?" he asks.

"Okay," she answers.

♟

He gets up early Saturday morning, his Monday-Friday 5:00 a.m. shifts as an urban arborist so deeply-rooted beneath his skin that he couldn't sleep any longer even if he wanted to. He showers, shaves, dresses, then lets Harold—Renata's 10-month-old prized Shar-Pei—out. The overpriced, exotic dog that some days Corbin would like to throw in the dryer and shrink down its ill-fitting skin and ever-increasing canine largeness to a more manageable size. Harold? He'd questioned when Renata initially brought the dog home. It's funny, she said, cradling the wrinkled pup on its back between her breasts like a newborn.

Harold's blue-black tongue, like a giant bruise, caressing the pale freckled skin on Renata's neck, beneath her delicate chin.

Corbin helps Harold out the back door with the side of his foot, then turns on the coffee machine. He can hear their orange cat, O.J., scratching in her litter box in the basement, which needs to be cleaned after breakfast; his domestic regime no different than his professional regime as urban arborist—the constant maintenance of it all. The deluge of flowering trees alone: cherry, plum, crab apple, magnolia, dogwood that line every other street in the area that require his dogged safeguarding, his careful preservation—he is, he tells Renata, not simply an arborist but a tree guard, not unlike the life guards at the beach. The never-ending upkeep enough to make anyone woozy with the relentless falling branches, the pale pink frilly blossoms slippery, treacherous even, beneath his feet. Not only is he saving trees, but perhaps in the process, he's saving people's lives. He reads the *Province*, drinks coffee, moves onto the *Sun*, eats six slices of cinnamon toast, then goes down to change the litter box, the feline putrid stench of it, he turns his face aside and dumps the clumped clay litter into a garbage bag.

Out back, he yells at Harold, whom, without the proper early socialization that Renata neglected, has become distant, remote, if not outright stubborn and strong-willed. Harold is in the unkempt garden Corbin planted last year for Renata. Her rogue dog pays him no mind, is busy uprooting decomposed beets or woody carrots or something in the fertile soil he imported from a U-pick blueberry farm in Langley, though none of the dried, decaying plants in Renata's left-for-dead garden seems to have benefitted from it.

Harold bounds over to him with a mouldy potato in his black mouth—the desecrated prize he has unwittingly found;

the rank odour a scourge in the early morning. The dog flips the rotten potato in the air, then crouches down on his sable haunches as it lands in a pulpy mess on the hardened earth; he barks wildly at it. Corbin doesn't know why. Perhaps trying to play with it? Make it whole again? Good flipping luck with that. Corbin kicks the potato shrapnel with his purple Crocs, tries to distract Harold from it, but the Shar-Pei doesn't budge. Corbin leaves him to it, goes back into the house.

After what seems like hours of numbing silence in their stagnant house, he goes to the bedroom door.

"Renata, get up and come talk to me."

Renata opens her eyes to the murky light, Corbin standing at the foot of their bed.

"What time is it?" she asks.

Corbin checks his watch.

"6:53."

"Okay," she answers, easier to give in than to start the day in a snarl.

♟

Renata's job in Human Resources is such that it requires a constant stream of steady decisions. A heady stream of conscience-ness on *Who* should go *Where? What* department manager is best suited to *Which* store? *Where* can she foist off the produce manager accused of stalking one of his female employees? *When* will she find a front-end supervisor that can handle the rowdy cashiers at Metrotown? And the latest: *Why* the Abbotsford store manager hired the Islamic hijab-wearing cashier, who is presently seated in front of her?

Renata smiles at the girl, she doesn't smile back. The issue not being Islamic, far from it, Save-on-Foods is an equal opportunity employer. The fracas: the girl's refusal to remove the black pashmina veil that covers her head and neck, intensifying her heavy-lashed, fundamentalist eyes that glitter darkly on her oval face like Middle Eastern oil on Pacific sea water.

"This is my heritage, I am a *believing* woman," the girl explains, careful not to insert the word religion or Qur'an at this tender stage of negotiations, but if pressed, Renata guesses, she will and likely much more.

"We are liberated women. We are not sex objects," says the girl, sitting stiff, erect in the swivel chair across from Renata's walnut desk.

"Well, yes, I can see that," Renata says.

The girl's headgear not unlike the stark babushka her Russian grandmother used to wear. No one ever accused her grandmother of being a sex object.

"It is meant to preserve the dignity of women, meant to *liberate,* and *not,* as Westerners think—to oppress," the obviously university-educated girl says with such fervour that she inadvertently spits on Renata's outstretched hands.

Renata withdraws her hands, discreetly wipes them on her organdy skirt that matches her pale pink-frilly blouse, the skirt short but not overly so, Corbin-approved.

"Does that apply to the men?" Renata asks, although she knows it doesn't.

"We are talking about men now?" The girl is in full attack mode.

"No, we are not," says Renata, resuming her professional H.R. face.

The girl's face is dark, intent. Renata surveys the otherwise mandatory Save-on uniform the girl is wearing: the white smock, synthetic blue pants, the polyester/pashmina clash of cultures.

"You realize Save-on has a no-hat policy?" she says.

"This is not the same," says the girl, meeting Renata's eye.

"It would be no different if you were a Catholic nun. You still wouldn't be allowed the headdress thing."

"Hijab," the girl says.

The girl goes on to explain: the *believing* woman that she is, as differentiated from the streetwalkers. Renata senses they are nearing the part where Human Resources becomes Human Rights. Does the girl mean the regular-going customers that walk the street and shop at Save-on? Or does she mean the real streetwalkers, like those on Hastings? Renata inquires. The Islamic girl doesn't answer.

"Well, we have a Muslim woman who works in Customer Service at our Highgate store." Renata says. "She doesn't wear the hajib thing."

"Hijab."

"Yes. What about her?" asks Renata.

"How old?" the girl inquires.

"I don't know, mid-to-late-forties perhaps."

The girl waves her fine-boned hand in the air.

"She is not required. She is well past the sex object stage. There is no fear of confusing…" The girl stops, no doubt seeing the furrowed lines on Renata's mid-to-late-forties forehead.

"There are only two distinctions for women?" Renata asks. "Believer or streetwalker?"

The girl stares defiantly at her. Her lips curved up like a kirpan. Not the same religion, Renata knows, but all the same, there are no hats, no babushkas, no hijabs, no knives either for that matter, be it the Sikhs or the Hell's Angels that shop their

Burnaby store as per the metal detectors they had to install. If she allows this, then she'll have to let her Russian grandmother work the deli counter, the Catholic nuns carry out groceries, and then the white gangstas on the front end will want to wear their wide-brimmed baseball caps, and the two Goths in the meat department will lose control and paint black circles around their eyes, and all the cashiers from Metrotown will be clamouring, ripping the discreet bandages they are required to wear over their pierced eyebrows, the diamond studs in their noses, and multiple silver rings in their pink lips. Really, where does it end? Everyone defined by something, someone.

"Don't you think that's a bit of a stinky choice?" Renata asks in reference to believer or streetwalker. She gazes across the desk at the young girl's confident, so-sure face, hoping for that small shade of heroism, that slow burning light of valour, the slightest bravery, a cultural pluckiness that could open this conversation wide, perhaps allow this girl an individual choice instead. She sees none.

"Are you very sure about this?" Renata asks.

The liberated girl nods her veiled head.

"Go back to work, I'll talk to your store manager," Renata says.

The girl rises, thrusts her chin out uncertainly beneath the veil, offers her hand like royalty, which Renata doesn't know what to do with. She grasps it feebly, waggles it up and down, and then releases the girl. Out her office window, Renata watches the girl walk across the concrete parking lot to her Jetta convertible that has the top down.

▲

Corbin, who's on mandatory holidays, has been at home for a few weeks. Thus far he has constructed a Berber carpet high-rise for O.J., reorganized the basement for the third time this year, and begun dog training with Harold, who up until now, would not cross the room even if his shirt pockets were stuffed with pork tenderloin. But now he's got the pup attentive, ready to go like Corbin himself every morning at 6:53 a.m. when all Renata would like to do is sleep until 10:00 or noon even, and yet she rises.

She'll go anywhere; do anything so long as it doesn't require choice on her part, much simpler to comply than to have to make yet another onerous decision. She gets far too much of that at work. And despite the sporadic body-sniffing inspections for which she's usually half-cut—still, she likes the idea that Corbin is the man of the house, her man that runs the weekend show. She hauls her sleepy carcass to the kitchen table, doesn't bother to check the rooster clock on the kitchen wall. She can tell by the muddy light outside.

"Watch this," Corbin says.

He raises his hand in the air; Harold follows his hand, and then, on the snap of Corbin's fingers, sits dutifully on their cork floor. Corbin looks at Renata for approval. Renata pours a slug of Hennessy and half and half cream into her coffee.

"Bad habit," says Corbin, who quit drinking a decade ago.

"Uh huh," Renata says.

"No, seriously, watch this."

Corbin gets up from the table, takes a strip of bacon he has fried up especially for the dog, drapes it over Harold's nose. Harold doesn't take his eyes off the too-good-to-be-true prize as Corbin walks out of the room. Surely not, Renata thinks. She waits, hopes her sweet, rogue pup will devour the treat but Harold remains still, every muscle beneath his loose, expensive skin stiffened, alert. Renata hears Corbin snap his fingers from down the hall. Her beloved Harold/pup/child jerks the bacon in the air, then down his dark throat. Corbin comes back into the kitchen, his face beaming. Renata can't believe it. She picks up Harold, wraps him beneath her housecoat and smothers him against her naked skin, his horse-coat fur rough to her touch, sends a seismic shudder down her vertebra.

♟

The next week at work Renata fields calls from the Abbottsford store in the form of across-the-board, uniformly pissed-off employees. How come *she* gets to wear a hat?

"It's not a hat," Renata explains. "It's a hijab. It's a religious thing."

Then the onslaught of outraged customers, mostly women, Westerners, who think that the girl is culturally (!) morally (!) and more to the point—patriarchally (!) oppressed; in contrast to the western patriarchal of Save-on men who don't seem to care as long the Islamic girl rings their Hungry-Man Frozen Entrees and 2-litre bottles of Pepsi through properly.

To the women, Renata responds, "No, it's the exact opposite. The girl *is* liberated. She is *not* a sex object. She is *free*."

The women reply: "What about the men, shouldn't the same rules apply to them?"

"The men are required to avert their eyes," Renata explains.

Big deal, the women say. Big flipping deal.

Renata sighs on the other end of the receiver. After she hangs up the phone, all she hears in her workplace mind: *Is.*

*Not. Free.* The Save-on World a repressed nightmare on all sides.

She opens her email, sees an upcoming seminar on the Sunshine Coast: Ethnicity and Religion in the World Workplace. How appropriate. She could use a weekend away.

♠

The entire week before the seminar on the Sunshine Coast, Corbin is cantankerous and argumentative, which Renata manages to circumvent by working late—then, the Thursday night prior, she watches movies she recorded on their PVR and drinks red wine on their sable leather sofa, the exact colour of Harold, who is tucked securely behind her knees. After the third movie, Corbin goes to bed; Renata clicks the television off, remains on the sofa with Harold for warmth.

Come morning, Corbin is sullen, has nothing to say as he hauls Renata's lime green luggage out to her Ford Escape.

"I'll see you Sunday night," he says, dropping her at Horseshoe Bay; that inevitable mix of contempt and abandonment on Corbin's face that Renata tries to ignore but never quite manages to. Those rare, infrequent times she leaves Corbin, she's usually so pissed off, she can hardly enjoy herself. Perhaps that's the point. It never occurred to her before. Certainly not abusive but controlling nonetheless in Corbin's belief that she *should* want to do everything with him, she *should* be his constant companion, his compadre, his soul mate. Shouldn't she? After all he is her husband.

"Don't bother to pick me up," she says, "I'll catch a ride home with Phil on Sunday."

She boards the ferry, doesn't glance back at Corbin, whom she knows is waiting for her to turn and mouth the mandatory

*I love you* no matter where she is—on her cell phone in the middle of a business meeting, standing in the crowded line-up at Save-on, knee deep in colleagues at Joey Tomatoes when Corbin is working late. Doesn't seem to matter to Corbin whether she means it or not, only that she says it on command, like a dog. He can be such an asshole sometimes, but so can she. She turns, sees him standing in the parking lot as the ferry reverses from the wood dock, the saltwater on all sides boiling and churning white. She doesn't wave, waits until Corbin is but a small unspectacular speck on the world horizon, then she turns to her weekend ahead.

♚

The seminar on the Sunshine Coast: Ethnicity and Religion in the World Workplace is soft on protocol, somewhat short of practical solutions, and downright wishy-washy in terms of what to do when actually confronted with the problem.

"Not a problem, but a *cultural opportunity*," says the seminar facilitator, her skin as blanched as the white tablecloth she sets her dry-foam cappuccino on. The vast majority of the Save-on managers, head office and human resources personnel in the room nod their collective, Caucasian heads in hearty agreement, no idea at all how to put it in motion given the current store policies.

"Something has to change," the seminar facilitator says when asked that pertinent question. Yes, they all agree, Renata included. Something must change.

Not having seen the sun all weekend long on the Sunshine Coast, save for the moody insides of the windowless conference rooms, the bleached tablecloths, the silver polished coffee urns, the Red Delicious apples laid out in third-world woven baskets around the hotel—Renata is twitchy, restless. Finally, the real reason for these weekend seminars: Saturday night in the muddy-lit lounge for drinks and forbidden cigarettes with the Human Resource girls, the store managers, and odorous Phil. An entire night of harmless Save-on drink'n'flirt that Renata relishes, the periodic letting, getting loose (not unlike Harold's skin that she so loves to bury her face in) that makes her feel more alive.

And come Sunday morning, the South American guy from I.T. that Renata wakes up next to without really intending to. Young, but not too young as to be inattentive to her human needs, so casual, relaxed, his sweet utter lack of control. She examines his unadulterated face, admires the smooth sable of his Chilean skin as he sleeps. The tactile of his beautiful brown fingertips, his full pink lips, mouth: warm, flesh, alive, the unfettered youth of him pulsing over her body not three hours ago, still tingly and present in her cloudy mind. The boy? man? Renata doesn't know what to call him, opens his eyes; they are green glorious green fringed by thick dark lashes; her cultural opportunity, her utter lack of religious values. She wonders if he counts as ethnic. He looks up at her in adoration, or so she imagines.

"I can't believe it," he says.

"Believe what?" Renata asks, lighting a cigarette now in the rumpled hotel bed, her right temple pounding from too many tequila shots. The liberated woman, the sex object she still is, the transitory freedom that sends tiny, trilling bumps along the surface of her skin as she gazes at man/boy beside her. What the hell? Her own garden long dead, the recent, fallen branches of her beloved Harold; and Corbin, Corbin is but a small, ineffective rooster peck in the back yard of her free mind. She takes a hearty drag on her cigarette that makes her head spin.

"I can't believe it's you," man/boy says, his beautiful face aglow.

"You, it's you," he strokes the length of her freckled arm like a valuable animal, the human resource treasure he's found. His multiculturalism. Then he moves onto other, more responsive parts of her pale-flecked body. No doubt he's admired her from afar for some time, she thinks. Funny she never noticed him before. But there's no sniffing, no smelling. No control whatsoever. He smells clean like the sea air, worldly like Renata feels in the moment.

"Wonderful," she says, taking his brown penis in her white hand, she strokes it until it releases. Afterward she glances at the alarm clock, 6:57 a.m. It doesn't matter. She curls herself around his relaxed, satiated body, falls back asleep. When she rises again at noon, man/boy is gone. She can't bring herself to shower the brackish smell off; she wants to savour the ethnicity of him a bit longer.

♠

Corbin misses her like hell. He hadn't realized how utterly alone and lonely the house was without her pink-frilly presence underfoot. Saturday morning, he sits a long while at the kitchen table drinking coffee, doing nothing but stare out at the dead garden, missing Renata. O.J. swirls about his legs, Harold tracks his every move due to the supply of bacon strips in his breast pocket. Corbin goes outside, relieves himself off the back deck, the loose-skinned pup watching the steady stream of dense yellow piss that smells off even to him, surely to the dog's keen nose? DSB, he thinks, (dreaded sperm build-up) or perhaps simply too much coffee. Corbin goes back into the house and fills a Coke bottle with chlorinated tap water, chugs it down.

Then he gets to work on the cedar hedge that runs the length of their back yard. With stepladder and hedge trimmers, he spends the better part of Saturday reinforcing the ten-foot-high hedge into textbook Roman columns, beautiful, cylindrical, so that when he stands back to admire them, he sees the appalling contrast of Renata's lifeless garden.

The lowered sun in the sky, the first hint of cooling dark, he goes into the quiet house to call Renata. Harold close at his heels, he almost trips over the cumbersome dog as he calls the hotel, but then bends absently, apologetically to stroke the dog's loose, coarse coat, pleasant in his calloused hands. The dog's head, like a miniature hippopotamus, his black muzzle slick with drool but Corbin doesn't mind. The phone in Renata's hotel room rings empty on the Sunshine Coast. He puts down the receiver, looks at the dog.

The Shar-Pei cocks his large head at him, waits for a bacon strip, which Corbin pulls out of his pocket and lays across the Harold's nose, then times a full minute, both he and Harold staring at the slowly moving second hand on the rooster clock before he snaps his fingers. Harold devours the bacon in one violent snap.

Corbin melts some cheese on bread in the broiler, makes a pot of Earl Grey tea, watches CNN until late, then calls Renata's hotel again. No answer. He paces around the house until he realizes that he's pacing in circles, Harold dizzy at his feet. He goes into the bathroom, opens the cabinet door for the scent of Renata's pomegranate body lotion, inhales deeply.

He allows Harold to sleep on the floor beside him, the lightweight comfort of O.J., an orange glow at Corbin's feet. No one gets much sleep.

The next morning, early before the sun has hit the distant horizon, he attacks Renata's garden with a renewed vengeance, determined to get it into some kind of shape before she returns that evening. Perhaps she can start fresh, resume the ownership that he so desperately wants her to.

♠

He knows instinctively the moment Renata walks through the door late Sunday evening, Phil's malodorous stench, and something else, too, some physiological, emotional change that punctures the stale air as she tosses her lime luggage onto their fawn sofa, announces that she's going straight to bed. He resists the urge to make her lie down on the sofa, remove her clothing, his obsessive, compulsive ritual, the possessiveness he's determined to get a handle on.

"All right," he says.

Renata looks at him.

"You all right?" she asks.

"Tired," he says, resists adding *lonely*. "Did you see the garden?" he asks.

Renata glances out their living room window, too dark, she can't make out a thing. She goes down the hall and shuts the bedroom door. Corbin waits ten, fifteen minutes, tidying up the kitchen, preparing the coffee machine for Monday morning, fills O.J's water, carefully portions out Harold's $80.00 a bag, vet-recommended food for tomorrow. He looks down the hall at the closed bedroom door, considers sleeping on the sofa, some dank part of him afraid of his own buried potential. He stands, listening to the silence he can't stand, the Renata he can't do without.

He lies, fully clothed, in bed beside Renata, who has drifted heavily into sleep. His flannel shirt dense with garden: the rich, black soil, the blueberry undertones like a fine wine, the desiccated plants he's piled in the corner for composting, will dig back into the garden later for fertilizer. Corbin looks over at Renata, mouth-breathing deeply. He wants so badly to smell her, not in a compulsive way but simply *smell* her, bury his love-starved face in her thick, dark hair, feel her pale, freckled skin. But he won't. He will not smother her.

As it is, he smells her lavender shampoo, the coconut body wash, and on top of that, pomegranate mingled with a truckload of nicotine, the boozy musk of spent tequila seeping from her slumbering body. He knows she smokes and drinks when she's out with the girls; a minor infraction that he tries to overlook.

She turns away from him pulling the duvet up over her shoulders. He waits. He doesn't want to, but he can't not. He slides beneath the duvet, careful not to rouse Renata, covers the length of her body, brackish like the coastal air she's come back from—for which he's always grateful, the coming back part, although he doesn't tell Renata that, doesn't reveal the chasm of his insecurity that rides like him like a sixty-foot Lombardy poplar in a lightning storm—that one of these days she may not come back. It makes him sick to think of it.

At her neck, Phil's flowery cologne that slides across Corbin's face like a limp piece of undercooked meat, no perceived threat, the moist cucumber of her underarm deodorant, the cool of her small breasts beneath the warm duvet, her flat infertile belly. He wonders if it might have been different had they been able to have children? For Renata he means. All he ever needed was her. He can't begin to know. His nose at her familiar hips, her hairless groin, her thighs—the trace of sea and strange man—the desecrated prize he has unwittingly found; the sullied odour a scourge in the black air.

♟

At work Monday morning, Renata finds a sullen picture of the Islamic girl in her hajib, hijab, whatever it's called, posted on the cork bulletin board. The girl's covered head posted up alongside the banned Madison Centre customer caught sticking straight pins into the top sirloin, the frequent shoplifter(s) at Aldergrove, the regular bouncers of personal cheques (all stores, many faces), common streetwalkers that they might need to be aware of. But that's not the case here, the girl is no criminal, or so implies the attached Post-it note with a single word scrawled across it: *Exception.* The purpose, Renata surmises, likely in view of their enlightened cultural weekend, is that Save-on is relaxing the no-hat rule; not exactly an across-the-board shift in thinking, more a glancing away, averting your eyes, turning your face aside so as not to smell the stench of unfairness.

The thirty-seven voicemails from the Abbottsford store she encounters before she can pour her first cup of coffee. That and her own marital relaxation on the Sunshine Coast, which sends a pleasant tremor between her thighs, causes a worry spot deep in her stomach. Man/boy walks by her private office without so much as a glorious green-eyed glance at her.

'It's me!' Renata wants to holler after him; the valuable animal, the human resource, the multicultural treasure she is. She can't believe it. Injured and grateful, she strokes the soft side of her arm to comfort herself.

That and the fuck of the day that follows: more calls from Abbottsford, head office, head honchos, Aldergrove Phil, who wants to file a Sexual Harassment suit against the Regional Manager that suggested he *Man Up* in regards to staff relations—all around oppression/repression/depression. Not one call from Corbin; his extraordinary silence.

🨅

Renata gets home late, finds Corbin morose, intoxicated, lying shirtless on their sofa watching CNN; he hasn't been drunk in ten years. O.J. is lying on top of his hair-covered chest. Renata looks at Corbin, he averts his eyes. She goes to find her beloved Harold that failed to greet her at the front door. The Shar-Pei nowhere in the house, she walks out into the night, combs through her garden, surprised at the lack of dead plants, sees instead the refurbished rows of fertile black soil that give her pause. She lights an illicit cigarette, calls for Harold until her voice gives out, wanders the property of properly trained trees: dogwood, plum, cherry, the cedar hedges trimmed in perfect columns. She goes back into the house, falls exhausted into bed. Corbin remains on the sofa with the cat for warmth.

🨅

Renata at work, Corbin rises finally at 1:00 p.m., his urge to urinate stronger than his urge to lie on their sable sofa with only O.J. for company. He pisses into the toilet, bothers neither to flush nor put the seat down, leaves the too-yellow urine, acidic and exposed for whoever cares to see. He picks up the phone, calls work, leaves a message about being late to call in, about calling in late—too late. He knows he's not making much sense. He puts on a pot of water for tea, pours Renata's Hennessey into a porcelain tea cup with tiny blueberry flowers painted around the gold rim, drinks while he waits for the water to boil. He gazes out across the yard, the perfect columns, the newly dug garden, the locked shed, the dog inside that gives him pause.

He doesn't wait for the water to boil, instead strides out the back door, across the meticulously cut grass in his Stanfield boxers, unlocks the shed, peers in at Harold in the dark corner, fettered by a leather leash, his hippopotamus muzzle wrapped in duct tape. Corbin cocks his head at the sorrowful dog, his own heart fresh with hurt. He picks Harold up, pulls the tape gently off, Harold's freed blue-black tongue grateful on his neck, his unshaven face.

He takes the dog into the house; the tea kettle almost boiled dry on their gas stove, the air dense with heavy steam, the shrill scream that floods the entire house matches his teetering, treacherous mind before he turns it off. He holds Harold in his arms like the baby Renata never had, the wife who's no longer his, his alone, his only. All parts of him dank now, afraid of his buried potential, Corbin feeds the dehydrated dog bottled water from a mixing spoon, then pours as much food as Harold wants in his dish. Finally he lays bacon strips out like a Sunday morning buffet across the cork floor; Harold's last supper. Corbin stares out the kitchen window at the garden.

♟

Harold missing Monday, then Tuesday, Renata, home from work early spots the unsettled pile of imported Langley soil on the side of her garden like a fresh grave. She kicks half-heartedly at the mound with the toe of her patent leather shoe, but her maligned heart is not in it, she's afraid of what she might find. No, better to avert her eyes; turn her face aside so as not to smell the stench of what? Unfairness? Fairness? She can hardly distinguish the two anymore. The throbbing pain she feels in the pit of her stomach like a self-ingested bullet. She sits down beside the mound of soil in her Human Resource clothes, thinks canine, thinks Harold, hijab, aware suddenly, irrationally of her hairless groin beneath her Corbin-approved skirt, her dark hair falling loose around the pink pale of her blouse. Her anger welling up, then her eyes: she can feel Corbin's gaze from the kitchen window and when she turns to check, he's there. He stares at her a long while; she averts her eyes. After some time she goes into the house.

"Where is Harold?" She confronts Corbin, who is back on the leather sofa, numerous tea cups, her empty bottle of Hennessey on their glass coffee table, O.J. sprawled across Corbin's hairy chest like a mink stole.

"It's done," Corbin says, looks her straight in the eye.

She can't return his gaze.

"Okay," says Renata, softly.

Corbin goes back to watching CNN as if the world's problems can be solved through constant monitoring. She goes down the hall into their bedroom, quietly shuts the door, climbs into bed without bothering to change out of her work clothes, the sun not yet set in the cooling sky, the locked shed in the back of their otherwise perfectly groomed yard.

A

When Renata leaves early for work the next morning, Corbin goes his computer, types in www.kijiji.ca.

Within hours, a single mother and her two young children show up at the front door.

"Really, you want nothing for him?" The mother says, her face bright, hopeful at this too-good-to-be-true prize. The children squeal in excitement as Harold jumps up to greet their sweet, innocent faces.

"He's yours," Corbin says, as he walks them out to their battered Dodge Caravan. Harold bounding alongside leaps into the messy van, no hesitation whatsoever. Corbin hands the mother a baggie of bacon strips.

"What's this for?" She asks.

"Submission," Harold says.

The mother smiles uncertainly, the two children hug Harold in the back seat.

"You don't know how happy this makes us," she says.

"Me, too, I guess," says Corbin, without much conviction. He watches as they drive off, Harold licking the grimy passenger window clean with the bruise of his black tongue.

♟

At work, Renata is confronted yet again by the picture of the intense, misinformed Islamic girl on the bulletin board; she wants to avert her eyes but she can't. The worry spot in her stomach a full-blown ulcer now; she can't eat, can't drink coffee. Chilean man/boy cuts a wide swath around her, disappears into the co-ed washroom, Renata's tacit tongue wagging with, "You, I can't believe it's you." Renata goes into her office, tries to focus on the mess of papers on her desk. She checks the corporate emails, same old, same old, she's getting older by the minute. The pain of Harold in her grave stomach so acute, she wants to throw up.

She digs a thick Sharpie out of her desk drawer, walks out of her office, weaves through the thrumming, half-walled maze of cubicles, past the Human Resource girls, past man/boy, who is noticing her intently now, to the cork bulletin board. Renata glances wildly around the stunned, stagnant room; something has to change. She scrawls in permanent ink across the Islamic girl's hijab: *This is a hate crime.*

Then she disappears into the co-ed washroom, vomits in the middle stall, wipes her mouth off on her pink pale sleeve, resumes her place in the office behind her walnut desk, stares out the window at the concrete parking lot below.

## Detachment

The dog attached itself to us. He bounded across the frozen schoolyard the same day the Grade Seven boys found the nest of baby field mice. The older boys dangling barely-formed, pink-bodied mice from their pinched fingers, chasing my asthmatic brother Aurum in Grade One, me in Grade Four, the screaming preschoolers and kindergarteners, dropping live mice down the backs of our winter parkas when they caught up with us. The dog, a multi-cultured, mottled-looking stray that no one recognized from any yard in our Ukrainian/Native/Hutterite town, ran haphazardly among the Grade Seven boys, the mice, us terrified girls, the too-young boys; the teachers barking stop and desist orders from the playground.

Grade Four English: I raised the pine lid of my desk; inside on top of my Language Arts book laid the cold, pink ball of a dead field mouse. I put my head down and cried soundlessly into my desk. When I got control and shut the wooden lid, which seemed a large coffin for a small mouse, Mrs. Michelchuk looked at me strangely as if to say: what's the big deal, it's a goddamn field mouse.

Aurum and I walked home after school, his raspy-breathed terror, my anguish barely contained, calmed only by the line of poker-faced teachers on the playground. The children stepping carefully around the debris of dead field mice, some live, most not, a Mickey Mouse murder scene. The adrift dog walked with us, only sniffing at the mice, not consuming them like mono-sodium glutamate chicken wings or swallowing them whole as in live goldfish or flinging them about for the wretched fun of it, just canine curiosity. Aurum dubbed him Larry and rested his hand on the dog's natty fur all the way home.

My mother spotted Larry before we even reached the RCMP Detachment where we lived in the domestic half, and shared our beloved Corporal father with the barracks separated by a flimsy adjoining door like in hotel rooms; the barracks where the holding cells were for minor criminals, the office, the six-metal bunks for the unmarried constables that worked under my father.

"Don't you bring that wretched dog in the house, Christina-Maribel-Madsen," my mother hollered through the kitchen window.

Aurum ran across our tundra-lawn to my mother now standing at the back door, her cast-iron gaze fixed on me as she nuzzled Aurum's blond head protectively into her groin. He choked on the October air, bawled about the horrible day, the awful Grade Sevens, the pink mice, his new dog Larry. I waited, glassy-eyed, only my trembling chin betrayed me; my vole-brown hair that my mother scarcely patted.

"You're a big girl now," she said, and then so Aurum couldn't hear, "Put the goddamn thing in the garage."

She gathered Aurum and took him inside the attached house. I sat on the concrete step, pulled out the silver pillbox with the hollow cutout cross in it that my mother had given me. Slid back the cold metal lid, inside: the detached pink ball of a dead field mouse.

## Detachment

Supper: My father, mother, Aurum, myself, Constable Pete (our favourite) although he had Tourette's Syndrome, not the swearing kind but a facial affliction where he arched his eyebrows, opened his mouth wide, then rotated his jaw like he was doing arm circles. Constable D, married, lived down the street. Constable C wasn't present. Constable B and E were out working, something about a safe-cracking ring, money that had been marked with powdered dye that stained your hands green.

"So the mice," my father said to Aurum after fried chicken, garlic-smashed potatoes, my mother's homemade chocolate cake with fudge icing that she also served to criminals.

Aurum nodded solemnly, his jaw wobbly, ready.

"The dog?" My father's eyebrows arched.

We stayed ourselves, two sets of eyes on my father, three if you counted my mother's, four including Constable Pete's. No daddy, darling, sir, could we please? No promise to feed every day, cover the cost of food, excrement removal, daily walks, nothing untrue from our mouths but our steadfast eyes on our attached father. My father looked at each one of us separately, moving his saddle-brown gaze over our faces, he lingered at my mother, the light in his eyes.

"You know the drill," he said to her.

Aurum got up, squeezed my father violently around the neck, and ran out of the room to the unheated garage. My mother sighed, rested her hand on my father's arm. I got up from the table.

"I'll go with them," Constable Pete said, winking at me, his brows vaulting high, his mouth wide, his arm-circling jaw.

♟

Larry: a dog like any other, ran without boundaries through our minor town, jumped the fence in our backyard, leapt through barbed wire, chased the Ukrainian Whitehead cows, the Anglo-Norman horses, the MSG-free chickens, one of which he de-winged, the pork piglets he only mauled. He walked us to school every day, chased the awful Grade Seveners and every other child in the K-12 schoolyard. Larry mouthing his way across the unfettered ground—a quick scent, his pink tongue, yellow teeth catching not only Aurum's and my hands but also the hands of the schoolchildren, so that collectively, instinctively, we tucked our child hands into our pockets when we saw Larry ripping towards us, his canine teeth a sharp tear in our thin skins.

♟

Grade Four Math: Mr. Predy at the chalkboard, simple addition/subtraction, the complicated trick of fractions ½ + ½ = (Aurum + me) = one (only). The new 4-coloured pen I worked out the answer with: red, green, blue, black, me doodling green monsters (Aurum, always Aurum) in my math book. The knock on the door, the hush, Constable Pete and B in their navy RCMP trousers with the yellow stripe down the sides standing at the front of the class saying, "We need to have a look at your hands."

All the Grade Fours holding their hands out, Constable Pete and B walking slowly, pausing to turn some hands over, Mr. Predy following along behind. Constable Pete does an involuntary jaw circle at which the children raise their brows; I hold them in my Brillo-pad gaze. He examines my hands all the while suppressing a grin, our infantile game of *Round about, round about, catch the little mousey. Up the stairs, up the stairs, in the little housey*—only he doesn't tickle my underarm like he does at home.

Then he leans down for a closer look, the smeary green ink of my 4-coloured pen, the graphic doodles I've covered up on my workbook so Mr. Predy won't see. The detached look on Constable Pete's face that I don't recognize from our supper table. My frightened face before I uncover my workbook, reveal my green monster.

&#x2020;

Supper: my mother, my father, Aurum, minor daughter criminal.

No Constable Pete or B. An investigation gone sideways. What were they doing anyways? The Senior Highs, yes, but checking Grade Fours for powdered dye that stained your hands green? Marked lunch money given to us by our safe-cracking fathers? Whose idea was that? Certainly not my father's.

"Green," my father said to me, cupped his warm hand over mine.

My pink, swollen eyes.

&#x2020;

Larry: well after the mice, the ink, the awful Grade Sevens, reinstated suppers with the Constables; Larry birthed nine puppies in the unheated garage. Aurum and I spent the glacial mornings before school in our plaid-flannel pyjamas and fur-hooded parkas on the cold concrete, puppies crawling, nipping, jostling, fighting each other for our warm laps. Larry, mottled, matted, exhausted-looking like my mother, no doubt from the whole parental adventure, licked her pup's excrement off the bitter cement. Aurum wheezing, crying every time my mother wretched a puppy out of his arms, detached him from his feverish headlock on Larry to go get ready for school. My mother sheltering his flimsy body in hers while I stood like a winter ghost behind them.

♟

Barracks: They brought in the killer wanted on a Canada-wide warrant. My Corporal father and Constable Pete, ash-faced, dog-tired, covered from head-to-boot in quagmire.

"A *G.D.* chase through a prairie slough," he told my mother.

Constable D on holidays, Constables C and B attending court. Constable E on lend to the next detachment. The Ukrainian guard they hired to watch the prisoner who'd murdered his entire family; the radio call that beckoned my father (all the town's father) and Constable Pete, dead-on-their-feet, out again.

"Lock the adjoining door," my father said. "Don't open it and for God's sake don't let the kids run roughshod through the office."

My mother's domed brow, Constable Pete's jaw gone crazy in the background.

"Bed," my mother said, shooed me off to our adjoined bunks.

She carried Aurum down the hall, tucked him into the bottom bunk; I felt her velvet lips, never long enough on my thin-skinned cheek, then she clicked the lights off, shut the bedroom door.

Later that night the muffled *bang bang banging* from the barracks, the Ukrainian guard's fractured Anglo through the wood door.

## Detachment

"I go home now missus, I go home."

The click of the office door as the guard left, the homicidal ruckus from the holding cells. In my mother's mind, the prisoner out of the inner cell, using the metal bunk off the wall as a projectile on the outer door. His soulless detachment, my mother's full attachment: Aurum huddled on our rose-bloom chesterfield, him clutching her poppy-red pillows, me standing on guard for him. She opens the door, prepares me with her steel-wool gaze, locks the flimsy door behind her. Aurum's mouth the size of Constable Pete's, mine pressed, bloodless.

My mother on the office radio, the metal blunt banging from the holding cell.

"Hurry hurry, he's breaking out," my mother stage-whispered into the receiver.

The banging stops momentarily. My mother's caught breath, the menacing silence, the listening murderer.

"The guard?" my father's faraway voice.

"Gone," my mother said.

"Jesus *H.* Christ," my father breathed through the radio.

"Get back," my mother said.

"Do what you have to do," said my father.

The dead ominous air of radio static.

The banging starts up again, louder, more urgent this time. The scuff of my mother's apricot slippers down the narrow dark hall to the holding cell.

"That's enough now," my mother said to the prisoner through the door.

The banging stops, the prisoner listening to my mother's calm, female voice. His mouth pressed inches away on the steel door, his terrible rough breathing in my mother's ear, her talking, speaking to the killer of families.

75

Interminable it seems, before my father, Constable Pete and seven other constables from the next detachment rush the office.

"Sexy," the prisoner said to my Corporal father the next morning, in reference to my mother's voice; my father's frightened face.

♟

Larry: the pups old enough to be on their own now. Aurum's asthma attacks the nine times someone drove up and left with Larry's live, warm legacy tucked under their arms, drove away. Finally, only Larry was left, lying in the corner of the garage having licked the cement floor over relentlessly if only for the attachment.

♟

Barracks: Me in my father's office, the pile of photographs on his desk. Aurum pretending emergency on the extra radio. Hurry hurry he shouted into the disabled receiver. Constables Pete, B and E—their seemingly effortless back and forth through the Detachment, our attached house. My mother brought lemon cake hot from the oven, brewed a fresh pot of coffee. The group of them sat in the outer office, talking, cracking jokes, my mother's lilt, the dark laughter of my father and his men. Me looking at so many coloured photographs of the decapitated woman, hanging out the open door of the ruined car; the black pool of her. The man who looked like he'd been tossed from some wicked heaven lying facedown on an abandoned street. Photographs of pickup trucks, like crushed aluminum pop cans, blurry figures imbedded inside, metal tombs, hollow cutout crosses, my pink cold mouse, my monster-green heart— the big girl I am now; the thick skin I will need to acquire.

# Detachment

Larry: walked us to school again, inadvertently, not on purpose, her jumping the fence after Aurum and I were careful to shut the gate so she wouldn't escape but she did anyway, ran headlong after us. Her pink tongue flapping wildly, spiky teeth ripping ahead of us the minute she spotted the schoolyard children. The swirl and squeal, our hands tucked smartly into our pockets, running, laughing, shrieking. Larry whirling about like a comic devil, whipped up by the frenzied twirl mass of children. Then the one piercing scream that cemented it all—Larry's fevered leap, the Grade Three girl's bloodied face, the yellow-toothed tear on her thin-skinned cheek.

Breathless: Aurum and I, the poker-faced teachers, Constable Pete in the Principal's office.

Detachment: my brother and I at the kitchen table with our mother. Why did you let Larry out? Well, then, why didn't you bring her home? My mother's angry face directed at me: daughter, older, healthy—not Aurum: younger, sickly, always off-the-hook, who sobbed uncontrollably. My mother pressed a warm dishrag over his pallid face to try and stop the flow; ease his breathing. I sat dry, stone-eyed, untouched by my mother.

We all heard the single shot outside. My mother rushed the kitchen window.

"Jesus almighty," she hissed through clenched teeth.

Aurum and I tried to reach the window but our mother shoved us back.

"Go to your room," she said.

We went down the hall, Aurum gasping air, me press-lipped, silent.

"Get the goddamn thing out of here before the kids see it," my mother said through the kitchen window, yet another dog-gone thing gone sideways.

Aurum and I on the top bunk, our faces pressed to the bedroom window. The backyard scene: my beloved father, his RCMP-issue revolver, Constable Pete and C in attendance, standing around like intermission at a soccer game. Finally Constable Pete dragged the dog around by her hindquarters to the front yard where the truck was, Larry's black pool, blood trail. My father stared up at my mother, his brown eyes burning with something other than detachment.

"We did what we had to do," he said to no one in particular.

♟

The next day Aurum got up early before the winter sun, pulled his fur-hooded parka over his flannel-plaid pyjamas, went outside and followed the dark trail of Larry in the morning black while I watched from the top bunk. From the front to the backyard, over and over again, paced Aurum relentlessly. And when he lay down on our tundra-lawn, his fractured, asthmatic breath delayed in the arctic air, his paling face; I didn't move. Instead my mother rushed out in her nightgown, her apricot slippers. I watched, my cheek pressed to the thin, bitter pane that separated us—my detached attachment, my thickened skin, my mother's steel-wool gaze staring up at me.

## Visibility

I'm at the mall. In the food fair, a mother reaches across the table and strokes her little girl's face with her hand. She arcs a layer of visible love across the toddler's soft forehead, over her sweet reddened cheeks. Love laid bare, I think, made clear. Wipe it on, smooth it over, and hold it in your skin like memory. As the little girl grows up and moves into her gawky sixteen-year-old body like a stranger to a new apartment, these observable motions of love will diminish, disappear almost in adolescence, causing the girl to look for love around her. Find someone else to hold her close, caress her skin, stroke her face—make her remember she's loved. It will be all she ever searches for if she doesn't find it. The visibility of love. Perhaps it's supposed to be this way.

♟

I drive down the darkened street. The willow trees are old and huge, weeping. They form a live swaying tunnel over the entire street. The streetlights produce fifty-foot auras off the treetops like hazy searchlights in the black sky. I squint through the windshield of my 1969 AMC Rambler and try to catch a house number. My mother puts her hand on my shoulder. "Stop here, Anna," she whispers. I pull in behind a light-coloured Mercedes convertible and shut off the ignition.

I glance across at my mother, her head is down, shoulders folded into themselves like fallow wings. The houses are all lit up along the street, the luminous blue and green and yellow of undulating television screens shine out their windows like the northern lights. My mother doesn't speak. She simply sits there in my car. Does she not want to be here? Are we at the wrong place? Wasn't it her that roused me out of bed not twenty minutes ago and said, "I need you to drive me somewhere". Where—she didn't say, but the phone had rung shortly before that, and she hadn't wanted to talk about that, either.

I light a cigarette, one for her, one for me, since we smoke the same brand. It makes it easier at the drugstore. "Peter Jackson for my mother, please," I say to the cashier. Like ordering a man. I'd like one Peter Jackson: tall, strong, responsible, likes to hang around the house—a non-drinker, please. I bet I could pick a man my mother would like.

We watch out the car window. A man walks by with two Yorkshire terriers, those dogs that weigh the equivalent of a can of Spam. The dogs skitter off-leash like oversized mice around the man's feet, possibly so they won't get lost in the thickness of the night. Like I think my mother has.

"Mom?" I say.

She holds up her hand and motions towards a modern flat-roofed house a couple doors down. A woman comes out onto the porch, holding the door for someone. I feel as if we are on surveillance. For a short stint, after my father's RCMP career, my father was a private investigator. He and my mother would pack a lunch and a thermos of coffee sans the Crown Royal, (my mother didn't drink) and then the two of them sat outside various lounges or high-end steak restaurants in downtown Calgary waiting for the spouse to come out and incriminate themselves by being in the company of someone other than their betrothed.

# Visibility

My mother and I lean forward in the car but we can't see. A moonless night and the streetlights aren't effective beneath the weeping willows. The porch light isn't on, either. It's like watching a silhouetted play in the dark. A man comes out the door after the woman. I press my face closer to the windshield. Why this house? Who are these people? Why did my mother stop us here? My mother inhales deeply on her cigarette, so sharp I can feel it in my own lungs. She collapses noiselessly against the vinyl seat of my Rambler. We watch the woman circle her arms around the neck of the man. The two of them stay that way for several moments like a still dance on a late summer night. The summer I turn nineteen. The summer I am looking for visibility. Here it is, they have found it. This couple has found it. The woman hangs off the man, and then lets her arms slide down his body. She reaches up and cups his face in her hands, then kisses him for a long time. The man pulls away and starts down the front steps while the woman leans against the railing. The streetlight catches the pink sheer of the woman's open housecoat. The housecoat has lace. I glance at my mother. Her head is down, she's not watching anymore. And suddenly, though I had no idea who these people are, I hate them. I hate how they make my mother look shabby in her grey sweatshirt pulled on hastily over her sun-flowered nightgown.

The ash on my mother's cigarette is long, unsteady-looking. I take the cigarette from her hand and butt it out in the ashtray. She doesn't look up.

The man walks down the sidewalk towards us. He can't possibly see us in the car. I can't see him.

"We can go now," my mother says quietly, not bothering to lift her head.

"But why? Why?" I ask, stubbing out my own cigarette, fumbling for the ignition.

"Never mind, just go."

I start the car and pull on the headlights. The man stops. He looks towards us like a husband caught in the headlights; coming from some high-end woman who wears sleek, lacy, non-children housecoats and drives a convertible. As I back slowly up the street, I see it's my father.

 **LEAD**

(led) – a heavy bluish grey metal chemical element that bends easily
(lead) – to be at the beginning or front of something

🏁

The summer the Norfolk reservoir flooded, the trees were swimming, the cows were standing up to their necks in their ponds like outsourced water buffalo trying to beat the 95-degree Arkansas heat. The cookhouse of the campground was under water, too, and Kade, one part salvage diver, (rare good money) one part Walmart employee, (bad steady money) full-part college student (no money), could swim beneath the too-warm waters in and out of the wood frames, glide through glassless windows, which he does along with the walleye, crappie, catfish, the hybrid white bass.

No spear fisherman, Kade prefers to explore the wreckage of the farming community long underwater (when they built the dam they flooded an entire farming community). Unintelligible to Kade as he drifts over the farm houses mostly disintegrated, mostly obscured beneath the fine silt like buried blueprints that he envisions whole, three-dimensional, thriving and full like life its ownself. He finds scads of Chinaware (years of collecting by the sheer numbers of it, best he could tell) on the lake's floor. Household items drifted willy-nilly about the drowned community, no order that he can find to the tea kettle setting on the metal springs of a corroded bunk bed, the numerous picture frames with faded, bloated, watery faces that he holds up to his mask, no longer identifiable, the metal frames stirred up by the lake currents like silver, gold, brass confetti floating in the clear water, reflecting glints of sun from above; Kade looking at the past in the present he can't find. The black-bottomed chili pot lodged in the American Standard toilet, the set of cast iron frying pans laid out across the lake floor like dance steps from a misplaced childhood.

The downed plane Kade located on his last salvage dive. Inside the pilot-less cabin, Kade saw the black and yellow lifejackets bumping lethargically against each other, off the plane's riveted roof like languid hornets trapped in a titanium nest. Someone had transplanted a spring horse from the campground, sunk the concrete, metal child's horse beneath the tepid waters for the divers to play on perhaps, or to ride the eerie soundless depths beneath the surface of the flooded reservoir.

He swims through the flattened houses and barns and chicken coops, knows them all like his breath, unconscious, involuntary. Kade imagines all the animals, the throng of Arkansas kin some forty years back standing on the high limestone bluffs above the newly erected dam watching the water rise over the river gorge, over their once-thriving lives, their own serried past. He can't imagine how they could leave it all behind.

♟

Kade hefts his air tanks unto the wood dock, the dock all slanty and broken through in places, shanty-town like the clapboard houses he sees, pitched like plywood tents on the sides of hills, the slightest wind a mortal threat. He lies back in the warm water, the weight of the tanks gone, watches the too-tame

LEAD

carp around the dock, lazily picking crickets off the surface
like fried grits.

Up above in the campground he can see the Park Rangers,
their new four-by-four (could be classified as a monster truck
but not quite, a few feet short, Kade thinks). The truck askew,
cockeyed, the front end dropped down into something. He
climbs out of the warm water into the hot fluid air, sees the
truck caught in a sinkhole on the side of the road, the hole new,
sudden, unreasonable, but to be expected with all the rain. Kade
watches the cocky Park Rangers gathered around the sunken
truck, off-duty good ol' boys, but on-duty assholes in their
beige shirts and army green trousers harassing the campers, the
recreational divers on a regular basis for their beer in the dry
county, the occasional round of pharmaceuticals (not Kade).

"Too loud. Why so quiet? Y'all alive in that there tent trail-
er? I'm fixing to bust your butt and throw it outta of this campground, you don't quieten down."

The whole campground congregated around the stuck
truck, the attending tow-truck driver, the red-faced, butt-kicked
Park Rangers. Kade spots Loyola, the woman who lives across
the street from him that he plays tennis with. Her sun-bleached
hair, the intricate ivy tattoo on her left ankle that is older
than Kade himself, but *still* he watches, wonders. Her hairy
B.U.B.B.A. husband (Butt Ugly Bikers of Batesville Arkansas)
at her side; he hadn't figured her the type. Loyola catches his
eye, lifts her chin at him in recognition while everyone else
shares a smirk or dozen with the tow truck driver, who's had
his own run-ins with the Park Rangers.

"Well, ain't that shit?" the tow trucker driver says, whistles
through his front teeth as he hooks the chain around the shiny
chrome bumper of the 4X4.

Kade smiles, shakes his head and gathers his scuba gear from the wood dock.

"Ma'am," Kade says, as he passes Loyola, trying hard not to wink at her, their feigned formality. Loyola suppresses a grin, looks past him at the derelict dock; Kade meets the pot-stoned face of Loyola's B.U.B.B.A. husband, his dull-shark eyes.

"Sir," Kade nods, losing the wink, the feign.

"Boy," the husband says, a declaration, not a greeting.

Know your place boy, watch your ass boy, don't turn your back boy.

A momentary shiver down Kade's back in the hot, thick air; he can feel the husband's eyes fixed on him as he heads up the steep hill to his truck. He throws his gear into the back, resists the urge to look back, see if the husband's still watching. He climbs into his truck and heads out towards Batesville where his great-grandfather grew up, his grandmother, his drinking father, his missed mother, his wayward sister, him and the scads of county kin, like excess water under his skin.

♟

The litter of billboards, a single one from Lyon's College where he's almost done his summer Chem course, Kade wants to finish his Biology degree in three instead of four years. The other billboards: *Stay in School. Stay off Crystal Meth. School Rocks, Meth Doesn't. Life or Meth? Meth Kills.* The latter tipping the balance of messages, the skin-scabbed, emancipated, yellow-toothed users/cashiers/shelf stockers at the local Walmart he works with.

Kade drives, one hand on the steering wheel, thinks of the light show he'll put on this Fourth of July weekend, fireworks at his expert fingertips: artillery shells, light explosives, his grandfather's WWII aluminum tags swinging off his pretty, hairless chest. The wife-beater tee he wears for fun, for jest, for the B.U.B.B.A. he doesn't want to be, the Methhead; the in-town country boy banging around the metal cab of his F-150 pickup truck.

He touches the metal tags around his neck, feels the heat of his girlfriend in his groin, and Loyola, too, similar, but different, the silent depth of her age; the unmistakable loneliness that draws Kade to her like cat to fish. He pushes the thought from his mind, focuses instead on his current girlfriend, who's tall, lanky like him but soft too. Kade on his four-wheeler, his girlfriend's tight legs wrapped around his thighs, her girl-ness pressed into his back, her arms clung around his hard body playing the metal tags around his neck, her warm breath on his bare neck, the cool swamp air like moss on their skin—the bullfrogs he and his girlfriend came upon by the secluded swamp outback his place. The frogs hidden beneath the surface of the deep pond, invisible to the naked eye but their noise (!) utterly boister-ous and obnoxious until Kade pulled his four-wheeler into the clearing—then the bullfrogs stopped abruptly, suddenly quiet. Kade listened in the absolute stillness, the transforming silence like liquid oxygen in his lungs, fresh blood through his arteries, could be the best thing he's ever heard, ever will hear. Then his girlfriend's hands dropped to find the copper zipper in his jeans, and his/her cadenced breathing in the gripping silence that he wished was his to take away, keep in a box for later use. After, when he started up the four-wheeler and re-entered the dense, overgrown forest, then the bullfrogs started up again, on cue, like Bugs Bunny's singing frog. He wondered who they sing for?

Goose bumps despite the 95-degree heat, humidity insidious along the surface of his smooth skin, in his truck, over the entire dry county, Kade gives in to the lethargy, feels as if he's going under in the hot, heavy air. 82/Pb/207.2 tattooed on Kade's right foot, the chemical symbol for lead, the sheer staggering weight of it, him, he pushes his foot down on the gas pedal of his F-150—the dizzying speed of it all. Do it again, please. For her, for light, for Loyola even.

♟

Loyola lives across the street in her fairy-tale, peach-coloured rancher. Their ten acres spread out neatly like a state park, hundred-year-old trees. Her three daughters grown, moved away, her B.U.B.B.A. husband home from shift work, not one of the three chicken processing plants in Batesville that half of Mexico is employed at—his is mechanical, big engine, heavy, dirty, diesel, dark work. Loyola makes him strip down in the garage, would like him to hose himself off in there as well but he doesn't. From inside the house, Loyola watches him walk across their rolling green lawn, a slight swagger, stagger (too many beers at the clubhouse, she guesses) across the uniform diagonal lines that she mowed late this afternoon on the John Deere Rider after the Arkansas heat waned three degrees. His short, swarthy body, like Fred Flintstone in his too-tight, less-than-white underwear. He walks casual, unconcerned as if he's fully clothed and out strolling, his haired belly leading the way to their peach melba mansion for a shower.

The diesel smell, the grease exhaust, the oily odour about him like a heavy, inescapable wake as he enters the coolness of their air-conditioned house, so that some days Loyola would like to sink beneath the flooded reservoir and disappear, if not temporarily but forever perhaps, she won't know until she gets there and rides the underwater spring horse that beautiful, hairless Kade told her about. They play tennis together. A tennis player in high school, Loyola's forehand is sure and sound, her backhand, certain. She might wander over after their nothing-more-to-say-to-each-other dinner with her oily husband and see if Kade's up for a game.

After the monotony of their same, stagnant unvoiced dinners, Loyola whirrs about the kitchen, the hot slippery smell of sour cream fried chicken lingering in the cool air-conditioning, the dark diesel odour of her husband, she tidies up the dishes, wipes down the counters, the kitchen table with an almost frenzied violence. Her husband has his riding gear on now, his sleeveless leather vest with B.U.B.B.A. embroidered on the back; she wonders which one of the club members knows how to embroider? The crotch-less, ass-less chaps he wear that she finds impractical, ridiculous really when you think about it. What's the point, if in the end, you don't have your ass or your balls? She wonders where he's going. She doesn't bother to ask.

♟

Kade opens the door to his ramshackle house, about a fifth the size of the others on the lane, his land nine and a half acres short of state park status. Ivy-ankled Loyola stands at his door, tennis racket in hand, jujube green balls tucked into the left pocket of her cut-offs, her slim hips lumpy, lop-sided.

"Ma'am," Kade grins, holds the door partially shut so Loyola can't see the fold-out poker table that doubles as both kitchen and work table—the poker state of his youth, the gamble of his inexperience. She cranes her pretty blonde head through the dim doorway, sees the scud of photographs scattered on the flimsy table. The younger, potential pictures of his father that Loyola went to high school with; shocking to Kade that she could possibly be the same generation as his father, who narrowly graduated, and only stayed married long enough to father both him and his sister—then, despite the sheer number of swirling Baptists in the dry county, his father found the back porch and beer, and proceeded to sink beneath the arable, earnable surface into his liquid present, alone. The melancholy photographs of his striking mother like a stop-motion film that Kade, at age six, tucked beneath his clothing when he went to live with his WWII grandpa, the curled, sharp corners of his flawed kin pressing into his bare skin. Photographs of his older sister, whom he sees at sporadic parties around the town, when she stumbles across the room, holds his brother's face momentarily in her hands, tender, like the mother he didn't have. Then she goes back to her current man, current beer, current life.

The 5-Card Stud Kade plays solitaire with, the countless photographs of aunts, uncles, and cousins, dealing out the familial faces on his poker table. The dealt hands: three-of-a-kind cousins and two aunts beats your uncle flush, my father beats your mother, my grandparents beats the hell outta your pair of parents.

"Y'all up for a real game?" Loyola says, eying the card table, the photographic hands. She doesn't comment further. Kade looks back at the poker game that he won't ever win.

"Hell, I reckon, ain't got any other plans."

Kade rummages around in his house for his tennis sneakers, racket, a six-pack of Budweiser, but he can't come up with more than one ball, no matter, Loyola's got enough for the both of them.

The tennis courts three blocks over but no one in the town walks, there aren't any sidewalks, just the black asphalt roads soft from the heat, the cars and trucks and monster 4X4's whizzing by; isn't worth risking your life over. Kade opens the truck door for Loyola, then climbs into the driver seat, winks at her as he turns left, left, left in a matter of a minute, then parks at the red clay courts in the deep shade beneath the trees.

On the full-sun court, Loyola in her cut-offs, her bright white tee. She's got him running left, right, up, back, centre, left again until Kade's dripping rivers down his face, salty sweat flooding his smooth chest. She kicks his country boy ass seven sets to three. Kade looks at Loyola, her tanned skin barely damp except for the usual Arkansas humidity, a slight smirk on her flushed lips. He shakes his head, smiles.

"I'm gonna get me a drank," Kade says. He sits down on the worn bench. "Wan' one?"

She sits down beside him, takes the lukewarm Budweiser, cracks the silver tab, drains it in the silence.

"I got a whole wad of leftover photographs, you wanna have them," Loyola says without looking at him.

Kade looks at her, a tinge of sad beneath her serious face, their shared understanding of lonesome. He doesn't say anything.

"Don't have no need for them now, everyone in 'em gone. All my grandmother saved when they flooded the reservoir. She walked outta her farmhouse and didn't take nothing but the photographs, no chairs, no silver, no linens, no set of nothing."

Kade finishes his beer, envies Loyola her dead kin, his own kin like sluggish carp in the thick air so he can't forget.

"I might've liked a set of somethin' to remember her by," Loyola says, looks at him, her pale limestone eyes. She cracks open another Budweiser. Kade forces himself to look away, pitches his empty beer can over the high fence, which lands in the box of his pickup truck, then bounces out onto the black asphalt. He picks up hers, stuffs it into his backpack.

"I'm puttin' on a fireworks show this Fourth of July weekend, y'all wanna come?" Kade asks.

Loyola looks yonder.

Off in the distance shaded by the moss-wrapped oaks, the dense underbrush with the brown recluses, the poisonous coral snakes (red on yella kills a fella), the deadly diamondback rattlers, Kade sees Loyola's husband perched on his idling Harley, red and yellow flames painted on his custom tank. Loyola's lackluster wave at her husband, who doesn't respond. Kade doesn't dare wave; he can hardly take his eyes off the B.U.B.B.A. sitting alone on his bike in the dangerous shade like that. Kade listens keenly for the sound of loud, uncensored motors ripping through the town towards the tennis courts. He hears nothing but Loyola's soft breathing, the sound of the grasshopper sparrows like insects in the surrounding trees, the idling bike. Kade glances back at Loyola's indecipherable face. He fights the sudden urge to get up and make a run for his truck, knows he wouldn't make it far, doesn't want to be the first to crack. Besides where would he go? Instead he waits, watches Loyola for a possible cue. She offers none.

"Sounds like a plan," she says about the Fourth of July, his fireworks show, the uneven rumble of her husband's bike in the background. She stands up in front of Kade, tilts her head, and arches her back, as much for Kade, he thinks, as her distant husband. She finishes off her second can of Budweiser that she lobs high into the humid air over the chain link fence, and nails in the back of Kade's truck.

"You giving me a ride back or what?" she asks, hands on hips, Kade's face at crotch level.

He stares at the red clay court beneath his feet, the spike of ivy around her ankle. He can't bring himself to raise his head, not with her in front of him, her husband behind them. He hears the rip of a dark motor, and when he raises his eyes back towards the dense trees, the deep shade, the husband is gone. Exhaling, Kade gathers his gear, and follows Loyola across the excruciating heat of the clay courts. He opens the truck door for Loyola.

"I'll take another of those," Loyola says, meaning the beer.

The temperature in the truck even more unbearable, Kade starts the truck, turns the air-conditioning up high, then opens one, two Budweiser, for her, for his shaky body. Finishes it in one long drink, then tosses the empty into the bed of the truck, looks over at Loyola—her eyes on his face, no words from her lips, no expression across her moist face, she leans forward and cups her palms around the mouth of the air-conditioning. The quake down Kade's spine.

"No shit," he says, shaking his head back and forth.

"No shit," she smiles.

He waits until she looks away, then backs the truck up, drives the three blocks to Loyola's peach house, watches her walk across the lawn. He supposes what he admires most about Loyola—is her balls, her goddamn balls.

♟

Independence Day, Loyola paces their peach house, straightens the sofa pillows each time her husband gets up to go into the kitchen for something in the fridge. No discussion what he'll do tonight, he's going to the clubhouse like always, like necessary every Saturday night and she'll be by herself, wanting her daughters to call but not wanting to call her daughters in case of bothering them with her home aloneness. She hasn't decided if she'll venture across the street to Kade's, all his young friends, and estranged father that she went to high school with, his aloof mother, too, Kade's wild cousins, his college buddies. Could be quite a crowd. She reckons Bobcat will be there, too. Hell, he's worth the price of admission alone; she may change her mind.

She goes outside, hoses down the front step, the concrete in the stone-hot heat; Kade drives by in his pickup, his scuba gear in the back, must be diving today. She waves. He waves back. Her husband on the front porch now watching her like a hairy hawk. God, she doesn't get him some days, hardly home half the time, then damn near hanging off her elbow when he is. She waves at him too but he goes back inside. She doesn't bother to follow.

♟

Kade didn't mean to be so long but the reservoir was murky, cloudy, he had to double back and forth across the silty bottom before he found what he was looking for. Mismatched, every variety, white, blue-swirled, green ivy, red, rose, pink, yellow, brown-hued, black trimmed, collector items he thinks but he doesn't know shit, vintage or otherwise. So he collects one of each kind, colours from every county as he glides over the flattened farmhouses, the past watery land where his grandpa would've set up deer stands, hunted for squirrel and rabbit and dove, built his own bonfires, shot off his shotgun. Kade places the assortment together carefully, bumped up tightly against each other in the net bag so there's no space in between—so they can't move, jostle up against one another other and break in the process. One big heavy net/town full of something, he swims to the surface.

♟

Outback his house, Kade's setting up mortar tubes, tying, wiring fireworks down to the last minute in the ebbing light, attaching his homemade e-matches to artillery shells and fountains, the big aerial displays, fast burning, slow burning fuses, Christmas lights filled with black gun powder, the precise mesh of fuses designed to light one after another in succession, the bottle rockets and Roman candles he and his county cousins will light up and shoot at each other, their southern, July Fourth tradition, the dozen artillery shells he's rigged to launch one after another, and the grand finale—the succession of 500-gram cakes he'll save for the end.

♟

His college friends show up first, his father, who doesn't miss any opportunity to drink beer, his father's high-school tag-along friend, Bobcat. Kade's girlfriend brings cheese dip and an econo-size bag of nacho chips from Walmart. The flats of illegal beer stacked up like Lego in the backyard that backs onto the green space, beyond that, the secluded swamp that stirs Kade's mind and scrotum, the loud, silent singing frogs. Who else? Does his mother come? Yes, she does, able to maintain a civility after all these years, as adept at smilingly hollowly, as she is at the pretense of sharing the same space with her ex-husband. Distance is the key, his aloof mother sets her lawn chair over beside Kade's girlfriend, a sweet girl from the town but not much for ambition his mother says. She works nightshifts at Walmart stocking shelves along with the methheads for Jesus' sake. Alongside him, Kade reminds his mother. His mother pats his hand, silly boy.

"You don't wanna end up like your father," says his mother.

Kade knows his mother's hope is that when Kade finishes college he'll move on, set up somewhere nice where she can also move to later, enjoy the proxy of her son. His older sister fully immersed in the town, various men she doesn't bring home, the late night non-stop parties. Kade's knows he's her only hope.

His mother plants herself safely beside his girlfriend, good for Kade because he knows his father won't go anywhere near his girlfriend. They don't see eye-to-eye on most things, especially Bobcat.

"I tell you what, them darkies is somethin' else entirely. I knowed one lost her finger and din't even know it. Found it the next mornin' under the kitchen table. Sue!" Bobcat says, chugging the Busch Light he bought from the black people who run the liquor store in Jackson County.

"Well, isn't he slicing into a fat hog?" Bobcat says, watching Kade expertly set up the mortar tubes.

"Yea, he a somethin'" Kade's father agreeing, then eye-balling Kade's lanky girlfriend: "I got the feelin' she thank she's too good for us, she thank she smarter than the bof of us."

"No shit," Bobcat says.

Both in silence, dranking from their aluminum cans.

Bobcat's slow, sharp messed mind, the paralytic movements, the sheer nerve damage from meth, his erratic muscle function that cause him to twitch like he's being electrocuted but he's the salt of the earth, the silt of the flooded lake, he'd give you the sleeveless denim shirt off his knotted, bony back, the blue healer pup at his can't-stay-still feet that he brought in case Kade was lonesome by himself, might need some company, and he brings his own beer.

"Life its ownself," Bobcat says, lying the 30-pack of beer down along with the others. "I ain't got no more."

He pulls up a ratty lawn chair beside Kade's father.

"It's 'nough," Kade's father settles back into his chair, beer in hand, a fifth of J.D. tucked beneath his feet.

Some Walmart cashiers that Kade's girlfriend works with show up, the healthy kind, fully toothed, slight sludge around their displayed bellies. Light, airy, fun girls that gather around Bobcat and Kade's father for the sheer entertainment, their mock horror of Bobcat's wildly true mind-boggling stories of the town's underbelly. Kade looks over the gathering crowd in the growing dark, doesn't see Loyola. He'll take her set of something over later if she doesn't show up.

Then he sees her husband in the background. Kade squints into the growing dark, doesn't see a set of bikers with him; the temporary relief up and down his long spine, the shudder when he realizes the stocky-set husband doesn't need any club members. He watches the husband standing by himself in the setting blackness, wonders why he's here. Where's Loyola? Jesus to hell and back, he hasn't got time to worry about that now, he's got a light show to put on, though it takes damn near every ball Kade's got to turn his back on the red/yella fella.

Kade crouches down on the ground to attach the homemade e-matches to the artillery, uses the light from his cell phone in order to tape the fuses down one after the other across the plywood board. As he gets to the last one he sees the black leather-riding boots standing next to him, the burning red ember of a cigarette. He looks up at Loyola's B.U.B.B.A. husband.

"Sir?" he says, his crouched position perfect for a kick ass kick in the face.

"Boy."

Kade stands ups, glances over at the lawn chair crowd, no one paying him any mind except for Loyola's husband, no mind he wants to mess with.

"Sir?" he says again, wanting to take a step back but not.

Kade's face inches from Loyola's husband so that Kade can smell what he had for dinner (deep-fried catfish and corn fritters he figures), and beneath that the darker smell of diesel, oil, cigarette smoke, beer.

Loyola's husband doesn't speak. Kade can't tell from his face what he's a thinking, glances down for his balled fists but they're open, flat, empty.

Kade waits in the man's unknowable silence.

Finally, without looking at him, the husband says, "Don't take her away from me."

Kade looks at the shorter, stockier man in front of him, the ripple of uncertainty across his dark stubbled face, his grey eyes as flat as his open palms, his muscled bare arms hung helplessly at his side. Kade doesn't know what to say. The husband takes a deep drag off his cigarette, flicks it off into the bush.

"It's not up to me," Kade says.

"She all I got, boy."

Kade watches the man walk across the dark yard, disappear around the front.

"Hold up," Kade says, his long legs striding after him.

Kade retrieves the net diving bag from the tool shed, catches him out front the house.

"Give'r this from you," Kade says.

"What in it?" the man asks.

"A set of somethin' for Loyola," Kade says.

The man hesitates.

"Chinaware shit," Kade says.

The man stands a moment but he doesn't say anything. He takes the net bag from Kade and crosses the unlit street to his peach-melba mansion.

# LEAD

▲

The faultless dark, the thick night heat like water in his veins, mossy sweat on his twenty-two-year-old face, Kade runs the fireworks like the ticking hand of his diver's watch, precisely timed, alternating between artillery shells and fountains, Roman candles, bottle rockets. He touches the wires from the e-matchs onto the 9-volt battery and then the fireworks blow. The shady faces he can't see in the lawn chairs, Justin Moore's country boy twang *I Could Kick Your Ass* blaring out the four-foot speakers in the back of his F-150 pickup, his mother, his father, his county kin, the squeals, the fleeting caught-breath silence in the dark between songs that he loves most of all— then the fireworks blow—the wow.

He crouches down lights another fuse, the fuse catching, smoke swirling, the light of the last fireworks not done, lighting the way for this next one, this next generation of light, his grandpa's aluminum tags swinging side to side on his hairless chest reminding him who is he where he's from, his ramshackle house, his flooded town, the singing frogs he supposes must sing for him.

His girlfriend and the Walmart girls are up and out of their lawn chairs, shaking their country white asses: *Like there's no tomorrow, tonight,* more Moore, please. Jesus, it doesn't get any better than this. Kade lights the grand finale, the 500-gram cakes, backs off only just enough he doesn't chance any fire strafe, no flying sparks, no sideways shit. And the fireworks blow and blow and blow one after another in succession, progression, shards of exploding light in the black sky.

# I May Have Known You

The teenage boy on the pitcher's mound tugs on the bill of his baseball cap and surveys the crowd, all four of us in the wood stands: myself at thirty-nine, lips painted a persistent crimson, hair hennaed a deep, glimmering copper, my face no longer young and smooth-skinned, no naïf glint to my eye; my Siberian husky, one; the elderly gentleman who lives across the alley from me (age undetermined) who can hardly bring himself to look me in the eye anymore; and the adolescent girl with the straight moon-blonde hair talking on her cerulean cell phone. As the teenage boy looks us over, I see his eyes are indeed dark and keen, jarringly similar to my boy Zachary's, and part of me wants to walk across the red clay baseball field and the lifetime since Zachary left, clasp the teenage boy's radiant, untroubled face in my hands and say, "I may have known you."

♟

Zachary was the type of child that caused people to stop you on the street and say, "Oh, my god, what a beautiful boy!" As if life *had* equipped my son fully and completely—if appearances counted for anything. His eyes were large and dark, bottomless really, enough love to last you a lifetime. His hair an inky black that hung in smooth straight walls around the nape of his neck—only the cruel jagged line across his pink lips betrayed him. I'm twenty-eight, Zachary in my arms is two. I don't have a dog yet; she will come after Zachary leaves.

🔔

I stand on the stage because there is no place else to see among the throngs of people on the fairgrounds as the riders come trotting out in full red serge on lanky black horses. My husband, Michael, is among the riders. Standing next to me is our first, and so far only, female chief of police. She is shorter than me by a head, and older by several decades. Her face is handsome and tight beneath impeccable makeup but wearied, also, the look of a parking lot attendant or a tollbooth operator. Nonetheless, intensity ripples off her like a power plant—like Michael initially, like the jagged hole my son will come to occupy. I watch the thirty-two Musical Riders stream into the stadium.

"Daddy is on the outside, on the left. Do you see him there, Zachary?" I say, lifting him high over the heads of the crowd. But Zachary is elsewhere, otherworldly, his eyes focused, troubled. I lower him; blow a raspberry on his soft belly. He laughs once, loud like a seal bark, then withdraws inward.

The gold buttons on the uniforms of the Musical Riders spark bits of fractured sunlight across the faces of myself, Zachary, the female police chief. I force myself to look away from Zachary.

"Look at the horses, all the incredible horses," I want to say to the police chief, "and the men on them—their faces so excruciatingly young and unbent by life. Just look, will you? Can you believe it?"

Instead I hide my own wearied face in my son's sweet difficult body as the riders' flags ripple through the hot Canadian air. Their beautiful horses kick up clumps of earth as they charge the crowd, and I'm sure they can't possibly stop fast enough to avoid disaster. Time stands still, the crisis looming, inevitable. But in a split second, Michael and the rest of the riders expertly rein in their mounts and avert tragedy. Zachary and I remain motionless, as the dust from the field drifts over us. I let the tears I can't stop slip down my cheeks. The police chief glances over at me. Her own eyes moist, she bends her head ever so slightly as if to say, "I know what you mean."

♟

In the sixties, photographers used to go around snapping black and white pictures of strangers on the street. This happened to Michael downtown, right after we were married. He was twenty years old. The photographer caught him mid-stride, like those photos of movie stars you see hurrying along Fifth Avenue or Avenue of the Americas in New York. Michael looked sharp in his suit and tie and white shirt with a snappy tan overcoat. His hair was thick and dark, his face as yet unaltered. The sky, mirrored in the windows of the office buildings, was a dull grey in contrast to Michael's shining eyes that were riveted ahead as if he were on some sort of mission. Perhaps, I thought, the simple mission of getting from point A to point B. Whenever we went out together, people—more often women—turned to look twice at him and tried to catch his gaze. Walking with Michael was like a stroll with a celebrity, a breath of extraordinary air, and in the early days before Zachary was born, Michael didn't give the women a second glance.

But as it sometimes is with attractive people, I expected more: that his morals were higher than mine, that his ethics could go head-to-head with any archbishop, and that his intelligence was simply honed by the superiority of his George Clooney good looks, straight white teeth, and charismatic personality that drew women to him like Narcissus to still waters.

↟

We sit in the parking lot of the government-run mental institution: me, thirty-two; Zachary, six; Michael twenty-eight. Michael stares at the brick building in front of us. The grounds are rolling, green, immaculate, manicured. I turn and examine Zachary's sleeping face. Zachary seems oblivious to the pale serrated lines that intersect his top lip, impervious to the alarming fits of seizure every other day that make his eyes darker than those of his father, who is rarely at home any days. And always there is Zachary's propensity for finding dead Siamese cats or stiffened black squirrels or even the limp vole mice that the orange tabby next door mauls into an otherworldly submission and leaves whole and intact on our doorstep. Zachary pets them all relentlessly until I find him—our enduring game of hide-and-seek.

Sometimes he's simply beneath our porch in the backyard, or across the alley, safe and sound, tucked into the small wood structure the elderly gentleman built for his matching aluminum garbage cans. Other times I find him clear across the neighbourhood lying prone on some stranger's front lawn, his dark eyes intent on the colony of black army ants that form a live, moving shroud over his still body. Then I coax my boy up and circle my arms around him, and after a while he succumbs to the unyielding heat of motherhood.

↟

"Zachary's not properly equipped for life," Michael announced one night in bed. "Not like you and me," he said, drawing me in close to his still-fit body, as if that were consolation enough, like he'd already forsaken Zachary, but I pulled away.

"I believe in love," I said into the dark. I could scarcely make out the injured look on his movie star face.

"So do I," he said and turned to face the blank wall of our bedroom.

♟

At the government-run institution I stare at an open field beyond the brick building that has a random swath of wheat. Overlooked by city planners, missed by the combine, possibly left untouched by God's own hand? The autumn light catches the rogue wheat and the slight breeze in the air makes the wheat sway flawlessly. I can't stop looking at it, such miraculous wilds in the midst of such immaculate grounds. I glance at Michael to see if he's noticed the wheat and for one brief moment I think, "It'll be all right."

But then I glance at my Zachary in the back seat and think otherwise.

"It'll be all right," Michael says, as if he hears me somewhere deep in his still waters, but still he gets out of the car and opens the back door. The dull look in his eyes is that of a man on a difficult mission. I rummage around in my purse until I find my rose-coloured sunglasses with the rhinestones scattered over the rims and put them on so Zachary won't see my eyes.

Zachary rouses in the back seat and smiles his crooked grin up at his father, puts both hands in the air like a toddler wanting up. Michael unsnaps the safety belt and Zachary leans forward in his booster seat and wraps his sleep-warm arms around my neck. I smell him and myself, the Smarties on his breath that he ate one by one, colour by colour after lunch, sharing the purple ones that he loves with me.

"Mom's going to stay here and look after the car," Michael says.

Zachary hesitates for a moment, his dark eyes perplexed. Then he releases me. I face forward.

"Come on, we'll do a pony ride," Michael says.

He squats down and Zachary drapes himself over Michael's back.

Michael pauses at my open window. I can't look him the eye, so instead I see the unyielding anxious look in Zachary's. I lower my head, count to twenty to calm my ragged breathing. The two of them wave goodbye. I can't bring myself to wave back as they walk towards the brick building with the metal grates on the windows. I turn the radio on and scroll the stations, find a country song about a lost dog, or a bottomless love that makes your throat tighten and chest hurt. When I raise my head, I see Michael disappear inside the building with Zachary spread across his back like a starfish across a stone.

I get out of the car and sprint across the concrete lot towards the government-run institution.

♟

My Siberian husky and I pass the group of teens at the mall. It's well past dark, well past the time Zachary would be allowed out, and unlike these teens, never on his own.

"Do you have any spare change?" a girl asks, the prettiest among the group sitting on the sidewalk in their expensive leather shoes and designer ripped jeans. They are only playing at this.

"I'm sorry," I say.

I'm not interested in her, but rather the boy in the navy jean jacket and Quiksilver Tee-shirt and skinny plaid trousers with chains hanging from the belt loops. There is a dangerous slash above the right knee, although upon closer inspection, I see it's superficial—not deep enough to wound. His hair is black and shiny, and he has a small diamond stud through his left nostril. Perhaps him, I think. I try on teens like shoes now.

The girl spots the take-out box in my hand, leftover cream-filled, chocolate-slathered cannoli from the excellent Italian bakery four doors down.

"We'll take food," she says.

I pass the twine-tied box instead to the boy in the jean jacket. He extends his hand and smiles, his fingers brush mine ever so briefly, enough to last me a few months at least. Then he sits down cross-legged beside the pretty girl on the sidewalk and the two of them untie the box like a present.

♟

Around the holidays, especially Christ's birthday, which nearly coincides with Zachary's, and also at Easter, the second coming of Christ, I frequent McDonald's, Tim Hortons and Wendy's where the teenagers go to get away from their parents. I read my book and survey the packs of girls and boys, all the incredible young boys. I know it's a matter of time. And often, while my comfort comes from the proverb "seek and ye shall find," I much prefer Zachary's and my shared game of hide-and-seek.

♟

"I may have known you," I say softly to the picture of Zachary on the Missing Children's poster at Walmart. They've aged him using computers, so he looks to be around the age he is at presently—fifteen. The carved beginning of manhood shows across his cheeks, his lips are full and pink now, the jagged lines faded with time, but the eyes, the eyes are every bit as vivid as a boy of six. I'm forty-one, my Siberian husky is three. It's been nine years since my boy Zachary walked out into the weak autumn light not a week after I rescued him from the government-run institution. The heavy footprints in the dirt where Michael left off laying sod in our backyard; the crazy zigzag tracks of Zachary's Adidas leading to God knows where are long gone now.

Months after the hubbub died down, Michael moved in with his English parents who live in a good house across the river.

"This is not how I envisioned my life," Michael said, as if in some weird, warped way I did. "I believe in love," he said in explanation.

I wanted to reach out and touch the ghost of his movie star face, but his dull eyes stopped me.

"So do I," I whispered.

I see his parents from time to time, at the Walmart, Safeway, the odd Sunday morning at Tim Hortons, but there's no point in keeping up with one another anymore.

Later Michael moved to a small town in southern Saskatchewan where he married a woman with a normal teen-age daughter. The life he *did* envision, the life he *was* properly equipped for. But still, there's no talk of my boy.

I walk the streets and avenues, drives and links and cul-de-sacs, clear across town to unfamiliar neighbourhoods. I linger in back alleys, peer beneath wood porches, behind matching aluminum garbage cans. I frequent basketball courts, the food fair at the local mall, baseball diamonds. I live in the same house across from the elderly gentleman who can't look me in the eye. I don't blame him. I hardly look at myself anymore as I apply my crimson lipstick, dye my lackluster-brown hair every now and then to a fiery copper—if only to go back to a time when everything was more than anything I could have hoped for.

I walk the aisles of Walmart every day, scouring the shelves to fill my overflowing pantry and house. But mostly, I search the faces of strangers to fill the jagged hole.

"Goodbye, Zachary," I say in my head as I pass the altered photograph on the way out, but I don't believe it.

## In Search of Lucinda

My father, three sheets to the wind, floats in the front door of our house. With him the hot July breeze, the yeasty after-stench of the Airliner Hotel on Edmonton Trail: flowing beer, the darkened lounge in the daylight hours, worn-out chairs and waitresses alike clothed in a murky crimson, the standard patrons—mostly stray men—a few divorced women. Crown Royal served up like its name: sharp, golden, privileged to the off-duty RCMP, who, like my father who also gathered there. Circa 1973, the same year my father is diagnosed with the kind of cancer that devours you from the inside out, like how a pear ripens slowly and you don't notice until the dark bruises appear on his yellowing skin.

"Look who's here," my father says to my mother at the front door, motioning behind him.

My mother doesn't look beyond his pseudo-sober face, she's engaged in determining the velocity of my father's stinking Crown Royal breeze; not even the rank, diversionary cloud of his El Producto cigar that he waves in the familial air of our house deters her. My mother's Young and Restless (Hung and Breastless, she calls it) blaring on the television in the sitting room, her Peel-a-Pound soup wafting cayenne cabbage smells from the kitchen; my father's eyes are dark, glassine on this Wednesday afternoon.

Past him are two men in dishevelled suits; white shirts open to their sternums. Behind them: two extraordinarily tall women, exotic in a transvestite sort of way, heavily made-up, Marilyn Monroe blonde hair, legs that go forever beneath micro-mini skirts, unfettered breasts, globular, (no doubt the real thing by the faint pink of their nipples beneath their silk-sheer blouses), dressed identical like that ABC laundry detergent advertisement: *I can't tell the difference, can you tell the difference?*

My mother's face can tell the difference.

The dark jasmine scent of expensive perfume, these women not from the economical Airliner Lounge, but uptown, downtown, somewhere other than our neighbourhood. Their heady splendour as they tower over the two men, my father, my mother in her full-to-the-floor, multi-coloured Kaftan in a brazen African motif that my teenaged sister and I picked out for her on Mother's Day—so that when worst-came-to-worst, when life-came-to-shove, in the pinch-of-my-father's death, she could camp out in it.

"Dick," my mother says, offers her hand.

Dick blows a raspberry on it. She wipes her hand off on her African tent. The other man stands in the doorway swaying, waiting to be introduced to my mother, my sister and I. My youngest sister Evie, while not present, is evident in the shrill-kill of her semi-terrified screams as she torments the neighbour's bullmastiff through our chain link fence.

"Ken Gorbi," my father announces, like he's Monty Hall on *Let's Make A Deal*. The object of his extravagance: a six-foot something man. Hard to believe the women could tower over him until you looked down and saw the precarious stiletto of their high heels. The man's face nicely russet, early forties, not overly good-looking but his chest and abdomen so evidently taut, fit beneath his unbuttoned shirt like a trophy athlete, a slight smirk on his first-rate mouth, no doubt the real deal my father found at the Airliner Lounge.

My father waits for my mother to respond; she stares at him as if he's Monty Hall's goat, the donkey, the ZONK prize behind Curtain Number Three. My father ignores her, welcomes them in with a swoop of his arm into the cool dark of our living room, the curtains drawn tight to keep out the record-breaking July heat.

"Sit, sit," says my father.

He slides into the scratchy green chair across from our sofa, the synthetic fabric looped in so many tiny razors that cleave into your exposed skin like finely honed tools of torture. The same torturer's chair I find myself in two years from now when I confess to my father's yellowing face, my mother's slumped shoulders, that I dropped acid and that the paper towel machine at the China Night Restaurant on Centre Street knows how to eat itself.

The men, the artificial women drop four abreast onto our lengthy sofa, "as big as a yacht!" my mother exclaimed when they found it in the discount section at the Brick, so cheap it was like an inheritance. Although now the sofa's ends are ripped open revealing substandard foam and cheap wood laid bare by Lucinda the Siamese fighting cat we also inherited along with the neighbourhood. My mother goes into the sitting room, watches The Young and the Restless a moment before she turns it off, then comes back, drops cross-legged on the floor, not unlike Lucinda squared up on our green-swirl carpet like a protective sphinx eyeballing the strangers on our irregular-patterned sofa. My older sister perches on the arm of the sofa; the pole lamp and I stand in the corner.

We gaze at the four of them: my father's RCMP friend Dick Tick. Not so different from the wingless bloodsucking insect that lives on the skin of humans, says my mother. Ken Gorbi and the no-name women that no one bothers to introduce, their hard, professional eyes—though my father introduces the cat. The women pull at their micro-skirts, the red satin sheen of their XXX underwear visible, and beneath that the dark pitch of their not-so-Marilyn pubic hair. My father careful to maintain his skating eyes above the belt. My sister and I try not to gawk. My mother's face like the cat's when she has to lick her nether regions.

"Ken Gorbi," my father says, exhales a raunchy cloud of cigar smoke that hangs in the air like despondent cotton candy, "is the Guinness Book World Record Holder for the longest baseball throw from outfield to home base."

Ken Gorgeous, I think. I look at my sister; she's removed her eyes from the women and is involved in the self-examination of her teenage breasts beneath her white tee. Prelude to the future when she will grow her own competent set of breasts, move to the east coast, grow increasingly private, and we'll miss her terribly.

"Four hundred and forty-five feet, ten inches. A record he still holds today." My father's eyes a dark sheen.

He waves his hand, clears the circus of smoke from above his head. Ken smiles, his extraordinary lean, fit body seated before us like a man whose future is written in indelible ink. My father glances at my sister and I for the impressiveness on our faces. I widen my eyes slightly; my sister, mortified with the dimpled turkey skin on the top of her thighs, ignores him. My mother smiles at Ken Gorbi.

Then turns her flinty gaze on Dick-the-Human-Tick, her smile dropping like acid. Dick, RCMP like my father, father of three children, married to a congenial but meagre-legged woman named Janet. Dick avoids my mother's gaze, tries to make eye contact with my father, who is avoiding both him and my mother altogether. Difficult to tell where the best alliance lives in this moment. Somewhere between my father's rock and my mother's hard pitch. No Monty Hall deals to be made here.

All of us watch transfixed, captivated, as if by car crash, as Ken Gorbi's rented date kicks her black patent heels off on our green swirl carpet, crosses her go-forever legs, then squeezes into Ken's side; the parade of her cleavage a limitless tour. The enormity of her globular breasts sprawled out on the immensity of Ken's world record pitching arm. My father doesn't know where to put his eyes; he glances wildly around the room. I study the psychedelic vortex of the carpet, preamble to the paper towel machine at the China Night Restaurant. My sister worries the stress sty developing on her left eye. No one/place seems safe for anyone.

All of us watch Ken Gorbi reach across her remarkable breasts and grasp the delicate pearl button between his baseball fingers, pulling the deep plunging thrill-frill of her silk blouse together and fastening it. The woman smiles tolerantly, her teeth so straight, so white, so college perfect; I wonder how it got to this? Ken Gorbi flushes, the woman doesn't. Dick, my-father's-tick, winks at my father as if to say, *you see, now you see*? For what will come later, after the Wednesday daylight tea in the declining suburbs.

My mother's face the colour of rutabagas, my sister and I horrified at the mere suggestion of sex/parts/parents in the same room. My father's eyes fixed on the cat sprawled out on the floor, her back legs splayed wide, the lewd, delicate pink of her anus in full view as she toys with the black leather straps of the woman's discarded shoes.

"Coffee, tea?" my father asks.

He tries to rise from his green torture chair, but once he's down he's down. He falls back into the looped fabric: once, twice, three Monty Hall doors down before he manages to engineer his feet beneath him. Then he stands vacillating between the oppressive July heat, the conjugal smell of cabbage adrift in the close air, the decisive moment whether he'll remain standing or not.

He collapses back onto the chair.

"Help," he says, like that Life Alert commercial—like that aged person he doesn't get to be.

"I've fallen and can't get up."

No dispatcher in heaven, or hell, or earth to send him help.

My mother disgusted by my father, the sluice of laughter, gets up swiftly, goes into the kitchen. That's when the flask comes out, Dick-the-Tick passing the silver flashing flask around the room, the women taking short sips, the two men, long deep slugs. My father shakes his head at Dick's offer, puts both hands up in the air: surrender/defeat/no prisoners here. The four of them giggling like preschoolers, like my sister Evie, who topples into the living room in her pink sleeveless blouse in search of Lucinda the Siamese Fighting cat.

The room stops, the silver flask caught red-mouthed at the whisky-glistening lips of Ken's date. She tucks the flask between the derelict cushions of my mother's yacht, where my father will find it later in the bleak of February, the black of one night during the third round of his chemo; he'll take a deep anesthetising slug when he thinks no one is watching.

Ken's date stares across the room at Evie, my mother's prized daughter—long after the fact of my older sister and me, the oops child of angels, the freckled-faced daughter God never had, couldn't forsake, but gave instead to my earthbound mother if only to lighten her load. Evie stands in the middle of the living room, her strawberry blonde hair like—well, like strawberries and wheat. Her divine face, that rare-red-copper combination that will take her places, many places and men over the course of her lifetime, but here at age three, Evie stands strong and smooth and small all at once, her right knee skinned and bleeding but she doesn't notice.

"Evie," my father says, "this is Ken Gorbi, you remember Dick?"

Evie remembers Dick, who immediately stands up, throws her high in the air, into the twelve-foot ceiling of our hundred-year-old house, not catching her until the last moment, Evie's prairie-sky eyes wide, her terrified shriek. My father's accompanying *whoop*, my older sister perched on the yacht's edge, silent, unmoved; I watch with faint envy, so simple, so straightforward is Evie's world. When Dick lets her down, Evie wants to do it again and again, until she spots Lucinda's ochre eyes glinting out from the dark beneath our sofa. Then she moves like the tempest she is and will be across the room, and lies at the shoeless feet of Ken's date in order to retrieve the cat.

My mother comes back with coffee, tea, Coffee Mate, Sugar Twin, Parkay-slathered banana bread. She sets the tray down on our wood veneer table, retreats to the other side of the room.

"So sweet," says Ken's date, her voice startling, serrated: too many cigarettes, shared mickeys, whiskeys, men.

My mother looks at her, startled, but no, she means Evie, as mesmerized by her as we are of this woman, her high hair, high heels, all breasts and legs and susceptible skin. The woman reaches down to pet the cat, then with permission from Evie, who smiles shyly up at her, she traces her fingers along the strawberry curls on Evie's head. She smoothes her own young hand (her age not easily discernable beneath the veneer of her heavy make-up, twenty-one, two perhaps?), caresses the salient sweet of Evie's three-year-old face as if she can't quite believe she's real. The woman attends to Evie at her feet as if none of us are there, crowded beside her on the sofa, surrounding her in the overheated room, making her know she's the thorn among roses, the rose among our thorns. The hush in the room not like before, this one different, reverential.

Evie stands up, and much to my mother's horror, crawls onto the woman's lap.

The woman and my mother exchange glances. The woman's eyes real, not the indestructible Plexiglas ones she came in with an hour ago, but sombre, sober if only for a split second; chance, change from the same seemingly lousy dollar you spend over and over each day, never enough your entire, difficult life.

"What's your name?" Evie asks, making herself at home, twirling the pearl buttons on the woman's silk blouse between her tiny fingers.

"Lucinda," the woman says.

Evie's eyes go wide. "Like the cat?"

Dick and Ken smirk, my father shakes his head in genuine disbelief, the Siamese cat in the middle of the carpet still licking her pink anus.

"Like the cat," the woman smiles, dares to wrap her arms around Evie's small, sturdy body, examines the scab already forming on Evie's skinned knee.

My sister and I watch my mother: her clouded face, her intense, silent investigation of Lucinda, past the thick veneer of makeup, the false eyelashes, the bleached blonde hair, breasts and legs like a supermodel. Lucinda's eyes dart back and forth across the room at my mother; difficult to tell where either woman falls, where either woman will lie. My mother holds her breath like we do when we drive through mountain tunnels, barely able to hold our breath, then exhaling in giant carbon dioxide relief when we reach the other end of the day-dark tunnel. My father draws intensely on his cigar, holds the carcinogenic smoke in his puffed-out cheeks longer than usual.

My mother holds her breath, my father's cigar smoke leaking out the sides of his closed mouth, thin, trailing curls of smoke about his head—then my mother exhales unevenly in the cool shade of our living room. Across the room Lucinda holds Evie; my mother holds the both of them in her soft yielding gaze.

And here, here in this lovely moment, in this little strawberry-haired girl of change, you get what you don't, didn't have, you get love and heart and second chance, perchance.

Then Evie, having fingered each pearl button up and down the sheer silk blouse, hugs Lucinda once, tight around her long, beautiful neck, then releases her, skips back across the room to my grateful mother who welcomes Evie in her arms like she's arrived home after some faraway trip, overseas perhaps, possibly on a yacht; the dark scent of jasmine light still on Evie's pink sleeveless blouse.

## Snapshots (In Bed)

My daughters, Tessa and Sheri come faithfully each week, my youngest, Jana is in the next city over but neither one of us can visit each another. Tessa usually shows up late Thursday afternoon, (one of my off-dialysis days), the only time she can get away from the never-ending phone of her home office, but still her iPhone vibrates and she must attend. Sheri comes on the weekend, normally Saturday if her children aren't in out-of-town basketball tournaments. I am here seven days a week, twenty-four hours of the day, two years thus far—in bed, like that twist on Chinese fortune cookies. Good fortune will come to you (in bed). This year brings extraordinary luck (in bed). The gods are in your favour (in bed).

Although three times a week, (Sheri refers to it as my part-time job), they come and move me from bed to a brief, hip-jarring ride down the hallway in a wheelchair to the dialysis unit where by mechanical lift, they move me into another bed. By they, I mean the small, kind Filipina women who attend to my code browns, the medical term for adult defecation, and sometimes the two RN's who mostly dispense the pharmaceuticals and run the front desk.

That and the sullen Indian woman, fresh from the Dwarka coast, who cleans my room daily, wipes the bathroom sink down, and the wheeled tray for my bland, moveable feasts with the same cloth she wipes the toilet off with. (She thinks I don't know.) Subtle reprisal for her less-than fortunate immigration to Canada; the sobering truth of our global economy, the inadequate trade of human labour. All of which causes me to wonder whose good fortune, whose extraordinary luck, whose favour the Gods answer (in bed)?

♟

My own flesh and blood mother, flash-brown eyes on a high-cheeked face, skin like North Dakota, a body to be looked at for sure on any beach, in any bed. My England-born father, pale, sun starved, red wispy hair, the soft-spoken man whom I love, under the large umbrella on the beach, my beautiful mother on full display in the sun. My older sister: the dark-eyed beauty of my mother but quiet like my father. The prairie town we grew up in, Mormons and Mennonites, Hutterites and sugar-beet farmers. The party boy I brought home to meet my parents, the man I would eventually marry, sharply dressed, flashy-eyed like my mother.

Late evening, my parents back from the company Christmas party. The swish of my mother's crinoline skirt in the front door, the soft whoosh of my father bringing up the rear, how he shut the front door with a sobering click that one time. My mother's slurred voice faded in and out as she went from room to room and snapped all the lights on, as if she could no longer stand the domestic dark closing in around her. My father's booming English voice. My mother lobbed her sequin clutch across the room, her silvery purse caught the stark light and landed in a rebellious thud against the far wall—then the glittery slide down, down, as if in stop motion, the sequence of recorded snapshots I revive over and over in my now-idle mind. My mother on the floor, my father astride, his hands wrapped around her beautiful, promiscuous neck. My sister and I pulled at our father until he collapsed, a sagging mess on the hardwood alongside my mother, her sparkly clutch; then my father quietly mounted the carpeted stairs and never said another word about it. My mother sat up and smoothed the skin on her lovely neck.

♟

My husband to-be and me, him suave and pretty, glimmer-eyed. My older sister (the dark, soft one who later sank beneath herself into voluntary repression). We double dated, the duality of our shiny new RCMP recruits. My sister and I dressed in pencil skirts, heels, soft angora sweaters, strings of pretend pearls, seeded promise around our young necks. The warm summer evening I caught my mother in deep embrace with my sister's recruit, but never told my sister because she married him.

Parties and friends, the car accident I was in not long after my mother's indiscretion, my broken neck, near-death, the bright experience of that light that I should have paid closer attention to but didn't. The astonishing measures of the surgeons that allowed me to live—pulled me back from the centrifugal pull of that bright, easy light.

♟

The death I periodically wish for now (in bed) but can't imagine not seeing my daughters, Tessa and Sheri's sweet faces, so like my own, at my bedside—the warm innocuous chatter of their ordinary week that buoys me up like a woman without a life preserve. These incredible human beings I've birthed and am fascinated by. I can't imagine. I don't want to. Near-death not cracked up to near-life, the ones I love, loved.

# Snapshots (In Bed)

♟

When Sheri was born, she was so amazing, I watched her for hours, for years in fact, couldn't help but notice the same buried silence of my older sister in Sheri's dark eyes, which worried me. My RCMP husband and I partied, our weekend card games, friends, so many friends and RCMP wives in those days, the morning I rose early after late night drinking, my head pounding, while Sheri banged an aluminum pot against our metal stove, starved for attention.

"Stop that," I shrieked at her from the kitchen table. "You're acting just like a two-year-old."

The injured look on her two-year-old face. The quiet way she set the pot down on the linoleum floor and vanished from the room, didn't say a word, exactly like my English father. The day I grew up, stopped drinking.

♟

Tessa arrived next, those baby years were busy. My husband also busy, hardly at home. I managed, thankful for the plethora of girlfriends that also lived in the row housing. We kept each other afloat. Cold coffee on the front steps, the congenial back and forth of raising young children, your own, others, it's the women I remembered most: the long, funny, life-giving conversations over the telephone while my daughters slept. The unlit soulless nights while my husband worked the graveyard shift, the stale rye scent of him in the early morning, our daughters bounced between us on our plaid sofa, distracted me, clamouring for French toast or Cream of Wheat or attention perhaps, which I gave them selflessly (why wouldn't I?), the pong of strange women beneath my husband's skin. It's the women I remember most.

♟

My third daughter, Jana was born. Not so lucky. Her top lip split as if by razor, writhing on her tiny face like a wounded caterpillar. Born retarded, as is the term back in those days. Umbilical cord around her neck—that sacred thing, that fundamental bond between mother and daughter, that extraordinary giver of life—equally able to give or take. What it took from Jana and me.

The palpable flinch whenever my husband glimpsed Jana's dark, crooked eyes, the hairline scar the doctors stitched across her lips. Saw you flinch, I thought, though the hurt I felt deep inside whenever I looked at my precious Jana made me equally ashamed.

Then at age three, Jana fell headfirst down our basement stairs. Even now I picture her, no stop motion, no sequence I can interrupt like a snapshot, but the awful tumble, her black shining hair, her spindly limbs and otherwise sturdy body as she fell down the wood steps to the concrete floor below. I flew down the stairs after her. My husband flew to the emergency room with her small, inert body lying on the front seat of his RCMP cruiser. The further brain damage, the farther my husband retreated, the harder my hurt.

♟

Years came and went, circled back around on themselves in so many ways. My party husband, his string of strange women, though deep in my heart of misspent hearts, I hoped for change. I waited for it like a rainy day that never came. My girlfriends and RCMP husbands posted to places other than here, my loneliness buried in the endless loop of my scenic daughters whom I loved more than the beaded promise of pearls I once wore around my neck. The multiple opportunities I had for reprisal, for extra-marital affairs with both new and old RCMP recruits, for I too, had my mother's beauty, her high cheekbones but no wickedness that I wanted to summon. My father taught me that in his deft silence, his pale English softness.

And in the end, life's leveller of sorts, the equalization plan per se; my promiscuous mother caring for my father when he went blind, lost his hearing, then his toes, then feet to the wicked diabetes I also inherited. The snapshot crystal clear in my mind of my mother standing in front of him reciting his dinner plate in a wearied, practiced bellow:

*Your Salisbury steak is at 12:00 o'clock, mashed potatoes at 3:00, green beans at 6:00. Applesauce is on the left, Orange Pekoe on the right.*

Day in, day out, then the doctors lopped appendages off my father like tree branches until my beloved father died, three limbs shy of the normal four. One-fourth the man he should have been. My still-beautiful mother in the early stages of Alzheimer's now, by the parade of notes all over her solemn house—particularly telling, the one taped up next to the telephone: *My name is Lucy Burrows.*

Her time, like mine, also meted out.

♟

Things changed over those years, for Jana, the not-so-lucky one. My husband and I decided to place her in an institution; her medical needs so severe that I could no longer care for her adequately. For the good of the other children, we decided, though neither of us could look each other in the eye. Surely the wrong was with us? We drop Jana off, the sun full and absurdly bright, wrongly yellow for the occasion. My husband remained in the car with the older children while I walked her hand-in-hand up to the row of low brick buildings with the bars on the windows, the doors that locked from the inside out, not the other way around. My sequin sunglasses hid my overflowing eyes, the last time I felt her small trusting hand in mine.

God, please, I can't think of that day. I won't think of it anymore. I can't.

♟

With time, the hurt faded, instead, prolonged guilt, the self-reproach around our not-so-lucky Jana. It's the only way I could go on for Sheri and Tessa. How else? My husband faded into days and nights, alcohol and warm women, a karmic blaze that turned to cancer at age 37. I cared for him the decade and seven years beyond the oncologists' forecast. Then he, like my mother, also died. No lost love between my mother and me, no umbilical cord that bound us. I grieved him, of course, my shiny husband of so many years—what could have been, the grief of him and me, the pretend pearled promise.

Not the private grief I hold in reserve for Jana, or my soft, beloved father, but grief nonetheless. I will go on.

♟

Like me, Sheri and Tessa age, marry, bear children of their own, the most fascinating people you could ever hope to meet. I heard that in a movie once, and it is entirely true. Then my older sister developed a lump that nestled itself deep in her motherly breasts, and spread like a stealthy fire with too much kindling. I couldn't help but think all that forced repression had something to do with it. And she goes quickly, as quiet in death as in life. The slough of death in my life like hornets at a backyard bbq. I mourned my sister like my father, worried that my eldest daughter, Sheri will suffer the same inward fate of excess kindling. Of my original family: only I am left.

♟

I dated my RCMP brother-in-law for a short time, the two of us so mired down, so bent at the knee with spousal grief and life's sadness, we found each other easily, naturally, wonderfully. We travelled briefly to warm places away from the watchful eyes of our children, my own Tessa was jealous, couldn't understand the nostalgic pull of shared memory, the arm's length of better times, the yesterday promise of pearls. We travelled to places where the sun fit the occasion, a blissful but fleeting snapshot of him and me in the middle of the Nevada desert, a mammoth cactus looming in the background—but their harsh spines couldn't touch us yet, not now. But soon.

Six months into our newfound selves, my brother-in-law went in for a simple check-up. Some gastric intestinal thing he'd picked up likely due to travelling, different water giving him daily diarrhea, and soon he was fuller than my sister with cancer and was gone. The short of our brief happy life like tin shard to balloon, like my sister, my husband, my father, my mother, the dimming light—the terrible glimpse of what I might have otherwise had.

I'm done in matters of the heart, so to speak.

♟

The drift of years alone, wandering health, my beloved father's inherited diabetes, my now failed kidneys. I'm grateful to have my four limbs, Sheri and Tessa nearby. Jana lives in the government-run institution but I can't bring myself to see her (nor does my twice-fractured hip and in bed status contribute to travel), but for the barbwire hurt it inflicts on my shamefaced soul. I will be glad one day to let that go completely.

Sheri is her guardian now, some comfort there, while Tessa attends to my every need like a pit bull, and for that I am mostly grateful. I will not stand, nor walk, nor camp again at Waterton Lakes like I used to, entire summers with my parents, and then later with my husband, my girls: Red Rock Canyon, the black bears sifting through the campsite garbage that we walked a cautionary circle around. All of that gone now. Instead I wait (in bed) for my daughters to come see me.

♟

When my heart went last year (God's favour or failure of my own heart? I don't know which), it was Tessa leaning over me in I.C.U. I see you, I thought at the time, through the foggy pain that seized my heart completely. Sheri at the foot of my bed, sad, worried, but resigned, seasoned perhaps by her age to the ebb and go of this life. Not so for Tessa, her frenetic face wholly despondent, like my heart, at the impending loss of (me) that I can't bear to see. My daughters talking me out of going to that light, that bright, dazzling light that I've seen not once but twice now. The glorious light they always speak about, and it's true, like that first glimpse of your own children—the light equally fascinating, captivating, alluring. A light to bury your world-weary self in.

So despite my overwhelming urge to give in, release myself from this mostly difficult life, my faltered kidneys, my lost loves, my sore, sore heart, the daily diarrhea, my part-time job hooked up to a looping, endless machine. My red/black blood.

## Snapshots (In Bed)

For Tessa, I steady myself, and say yes to the opening of my heart, the stainless steel knives of the surgeons that make me live yet again.

♦

And I'm here (in bed.) Waiting for the week to wind out, the daily Indian woman to come wipe down my wheeled tray with the toilet rag, the bland food, the code browns I've grown accustomed to. I no longer suffer the shame of soiled diapers, the three times a week jaunt down the hall, the mechanical lifts, the circulatory cleansing of one's blood.

From time to time, I won't see or hear from Sheri or Tessa for weeks, and I know then that life is hard for them, some present worry (of which I have none now, relieved of that outside duty, that exterior world of danger, cares, general anxieties). My children and their own, sometimes wayward children that otherwise occupy them, keep them away from temporarily me, the sadness they don't share but I see it imprinted on their tired adult faces, hear it in their long distance voices—this double duty of caring. I know it like my black/red blood.

Now and then, Sheri and Tessa come together; they talk and chatter, laugh riotously, catch up with one other. I lie in bed and listen; so mesmerized by their familiar voices, our shared memories so imbedded in me that I think they are speaking inside my head at times. The surprising life of the mind. Their fast lives, so many things—worries that are mostly foreign to me now; some comfort there.

And when the conversation lulls, I stick my hand out through the metal side rails—my hand, which has curled unto itself like a fall leaf—and I ask Tessa or Sheri to hold it. (The dirty secret of old age is that no one touches you anymore.)

Their hands so small, trusting, (always the child), it reminds me of my Jana, and the grief seeps momentarily into my immobilized world then, and I catch my breath until the pain slips away—but all the same, it is the age-old comfort of touch. Their love that I touch, the comfort I missed.

I gaze at my daughters, the tight brave smiles on their faces, for me, I know but I wish they wouldn't. Just come, *be*, I think but I can't tell them that. They have so much ahead of them that will require their braveness, their tight smiles. Besides, I can't stand to see the despondency that rides beneath their pretend brave faces—the good fortune we were promised, the favours we didn't get from Gods, save for the extraordinary luck of my fascinating children leaning over me (in bed), tied to me like an umbilical cord. It's the women I will remember most.

## Pioneer

Caleb home from school sitting at the kitchen table eating Ritz crackers, marbled cheese, when I notice the ragged pink and orange gingham cloth tied around his Third Grade waist.

"What's that?"

"We made straw dolls for Pioneer Day," he says.

"Oh," I say. "Did you make a belt?"

He gets up, and grinning madly, does his scrawny-armed version of the chicken dance around the kitchen.

"Did you walk home like that?" I ask.

"Why?" he asks, his small face suddenly serious.

He watches me closely, measuring the odd question against my set face. He stands, waits for me to release him.

"Never mind. Do your homework."

The grin slides back onto his colourless face that everyone, including the doctor, asks if he's been checked for anemia? No, not anemic, just my son's pale, translucent skin beneath which I can map his every delicate blue vein.

♟

The next morning my son is up watching SpongeBob SquarePants on the television. He's dressed, has the pink and orange gingham belt tied around his waist again, and is singing *I'm ready, I'm ready, I'm ready, ready, ready* along with SpongeBob.

"What doing?" I ask.

"Watching cartoons," Caleb says.

"What doing with this?" I catch a loose thread on the ging-ham cloth and pull it off.

"It's my pioneer belt," he says, not looking at me.

"You're a goofball," I say, hold him tight so he can't break into chicken but he does anyway, and dances away from me.

Despite myself, I laugh.

"How about some cheesy eggs?" I ask.

"Yippee," he says, coming back to me.

His small pale body a furnace of fierce warmth in my arms. I hold him longer than I should, but he doesn't squirm his way out like his much-too-old-for-that teenaged sister, Cassidy, who walks into the kitchen, notices the cloth belt tied overtop of Caleb's purple-striped shirt.

"You're such a dweeb, Caleb," she says, pours a cup of coffee from the Tim Hortons machine that my husband won last month in the Roll-Up-The-Rim-To-Win contest. He had to answer a mathematical skill-testing question, which he put on speakerphone so we could all pitch in, Caleb getting the answer before the rest of us.

"Smart boy," my husband said.

"Too smart sometimes," I replied.

♟

The Santa hat that Caleb wore at the start of Third Grade, barely mid-September, hardly even winter. The other children, laughing, teasing, pulling the hat off his head every chance they got. Caleb undisturbed, wore it casually, didn't care, and by mid-November as I dropped Caleb off to school, the other Santa hats that appeared until soon a solid third of the students in red-felt Santa hats with mottled fun fur around the rim, the dangle of white fuzzy balls as they chased one another on the upper playground, Caleb with his group of friends walking coolly among them.

"Roll up the rim to win," my husband quips when I told him later about the Santa hat trend that Caleb had pioneered at school. My mother pride, my pros and cons concern at Caleb's funny, free-spirited, unflinching will, his who-gives-a-sweet-fuck attitude that makes him the delicate, affectionate boy I'm afraid he is.

My husband shrugs.

"It's nothing," he says, "you're worrying about nothing."

He pulls me into his arms; I relax into the earthly, mannish smell of him.

♠

For Crazy Hair day at school, Caleb comes home and says, blue.

"Blue hair, mom. I want blue."

We walk over to Walgreens, peruse the massive hair aisle, find a tube of washable Blue Gel with glitter sparkles in it designed for No-Fuss dos, Sure-Stick styles, guaranteed to hold despite gale force winds.

"Like this?" I ask. "Blue with gold glitter?"

"Yep," Caleb says, his olive-coloured eyes live with anticipation.

"Remember the guy with the green Mohawk?" he asks.

I do. A foot-long Mohawk, liberty-spiked for full effect. He walks past our house every morning in his skinny black jeans, pointy shoes, silver swinging chains, real barbed wire bracelet, dangerous green hair that he wears like strict camouflage, covering the lissome way he moves down the street—smooth, graceful like a dancer. The lithe of his long body all silver and black, spiked and barbed—all of it setting him apart from every other teenager in our ten-churched, conservative rural town. An androgynous English Sex Pistol flicking hand-rolled cigarette butts onto my suburban-dead lawn.

We walk home, Caleb's small hand tightening in mine when we cross the busy intersection. The large hug I get after I liberty-spike the front part of his sienna-brown hair in blue, glittery sparkles for Crazy Hair day at school the next morning. His sister Cassidy chides him about the blue, the spikes, the precious time required in our single bathroom, the goddamn gold sparkles everywhere.

"Watch your goddamn language," my husband says, winking at her and me.

I pull Caleb close to my body; cover his sticky-out ears with my mother hands. He smiles up at me, one tooth missing, the one next to it, loose, hanging by a thin, fragile thread, ready to fall out.

Cassidy rolls her teenage eyes at us.

♟

I get my nails done, an upcoming party for the company my husband works for. Caleb accompanies me to the salon, the row of small Asian women in a line hunched over the gargantuan pasty hands and feet of Caucasian women. Caleb sits next to me, dipping his boy fingers into the same warm soapy Joy detergent as mine. Extending his individual fingers towards the Asian woman for inclusion, a tender slip of Orange Blossom on his small white nails that he holds up in the air to dry, admire while the Asian women titter and laugh, the rush of foreign language around the two of us.

# Pioneer

In bed with my husband, our heterosexual bodies pressed against one another, mine racked with fear that I may be homophobic. Me who graduated from Art College along with my open-minded, but straight-as-a-narrow-arrow husband, both of us alongside the guys, the gays, the gals, the lesbians, the bi's, the tortured artists, the pierced, the mohawked, the suffering— all of us against the grain. But that was the point, wasn't it? The reason we enrolled at Art College in the first place because we were already outsiders, already blowing solitaire in the grainy field of our conventional prairie landscape?

The transgendered first year, Norman by day, transformed into Taylor by night at the same nightclub my husband and I used to frequent. We were fascinated by Taylor's perfectly executed female transformation—that and the straight male he/she was trying to pick up one night. The straight man transported by nine too many rye and sevens, so that the allure of Taylor's questionable sex went unquestioned as they waltzed out the nightclub door together.

Aftermath: the three months of Art College that Taylor missed that first year, his male face too blackened and swollen to attend classes. The swing of an aluminum baseball bat so severe that the newspaper reported the young Art Student was lucky to be alive. I wondered if Norman felt the same? Every time I saw Norman afterwards slinking along the back stairwell of Graffiti Hall at Art College, I wanted to walk over, circle him in my arms, tell him it was all right.

But I didn't, couldn't, because I didn't know him well enough.

"It's not the same as Caleb," my husband tells me when I remind him in bed that night; my husband's stiffening groin finding my cool backside.

"Nothing more than childhood curiosity." He cups his hands around my breasts like a living, breathing bra, the heat of his male support.

♟

Garbage Day, I haul our two allowable bags out to the curb, look across the street at the seventy-year-old Vietnam vet who has made friends with the pot dealers that own the house next door to him. The suspect house: the basement windows covered over in tin foil, the black puffy airy bags of garbage the pot-dealers carry out every few months or so under heavy guard, the six or eight hefty men on hand just in case. The Vietnam vet coming out of his lonely house to say hello, shoot the breeze with the puffed-up, muscled guys standing around the pickup truck, as they are this morning. The cheery, baffling banter that serves to further confuse my battered suburbanite sense as I stand on the curb and simply watch; the group of brawny men ignoring my innocuous housewife existence. How did I end up like this? Ineffectual, possibly homophobic, a mere observer of blatant crime?

Then Sex Pistol walks by right on schedule, on his way to lonely, tacit days at the local high school, not many of his kind in our small, conformist town. The specter of his green liberty-spiked hair like a flashing light on our suburban street—notwithstanding the anomaly of the pot dealers on harvest day—otherwise the rest of our street entirely normal. The teen-ager's silver chains a-swing, the barbs of his crude wire bracelet piercing his delicate wrists as if to remind him of something, some pain he might otherwise forget. The metal studs on his black ominous shoes, his don't-fuck-with-me eyes that catch mine as he's about to flick his cigarette butt on my lawn.

# Pioneer

The hesitant flicker I note beneath Sex Pistol's masquerade, his jugular pulsing truculent on his sleek, feminine throat. That brief, mistaken moment when he lets his masculine guard down, when the swing of an aluminum bat or the tender slice of a self-administered razor on his adolescent wrists could bring him to his knees, and if he's lucky—like Norman—he might end up alive, duly marked, and slinking along the back walls of his future life.

I want him to take the chains off, wear American Eagle jeans and Converse runners, wash the green spikes from his hair, cut the incisive ends off his barbed wire bracelet. I want him to move down the street like a man.

You don't have to do this; I want to yell after him.

No, that's not what I want to say, instead: Don't do this. Don't taunt the world, don't fuck with fate.

Sex Pistol takes a death drag off his hand-rolled cigarette, like his life possibly? Full, dark, unfiltered—unafraid? I don't know. But I'm afraid—for him, for me, for the colourful potential of my colourless Caleb.

I pause, unsure how to react. Smile, wave, ignore, step forward and betray my safe, normal housewife existence? Circle my arms around Sex Pistol's thin, people-starved, gay punk-wrapped body? I stand paralyzed by my domesticated fear. The puffy men across the street stop loading their illusionary bags of illicit garbage and stare outright at Sex Pistol whose icy, scared eyes meet the glacial surface of theirs. The silent hostile back and forth is tangible, hazardous in the cold morning air separated only by the black asphalt of our domestic street: social misfit, illegal pot dealers, innocuous, suburban housewife, the seventy-year-old veteran of an undesirable war; none of us finding a place to rest our flickering eyes.

No one moves as we stare at the deviant groups of one another.

In that brief, fleeting moment, rampant with the record of Norman, and possibly my future Caleb, I make my choice. I nod definitively at Sex Pistol, who refrains from flicking his cigarette butt onto my lawn. Although he will take three steps more tomorrow morning and flick his cigarette butt onto the stranger's lawn next door. He tilts his sharp green liberty spikes at me, the soft of his don't-fuck fated eyes. I wave boldly across the black asphalt at the pot dealers, the hefty garbage men who don't wave back, except for the vet who waves with all the enthusiasm of an oblivious tourist in our foreign town.

♟

Movie day: Caleb sprints to the van along with his four friends, all of them fighting for the bucket seats. I slide the door open, Caleb's first in. I see the gingham belt has resurfaced from Lord knows where, I thought I'd thrown it out at least three times over these past months, but here it is tied securely around the waist of Caleb's Tough-Kid jeans. I grab Caleb and hoist him back. His fours friends freeze behind me.

"Are you wearing that to the movie?"

Caleb grins and nods, presses his forehead to mine so we see one-eyed like a Cyclops. His friends laugh at him and me. Only I don't see eye-to-eye with him. I can't see beyond the fated-ness of him. I am cross and my face shows it. Caleb pulls back, the confused hesitancy in his eyes looking up at my fixed face, his friends inordinately quiet now.

"Get into the van." I release his waist, but not my face.

He climbs in and obediently snaps on his seatbelt. His friends follow. I drive the short distance into the city to the movie theatre in silence, the rough mountains in the distance, the mountain of my anger, the underwater SpongeBob depth of my fear.

When we get to the theatre Caleb slinks out of the van, his friends bouncing around him as they always do, obvious that none of them notice or even care about the gingham belt that sets him apart, marks him for life possibly. Only me.

"Cold out," I say as I slide the zipper up on Caleb's hoodie, but he's on to me now.

He tugs the zipper back down defiantly to reveal his ragged belt. I leave it be.

Inside the theatre: popcorn, Rolos, root beer, multiple buddy trips to the bathroom and we are seated in the front row. Caleb unusually quiet well behaved. The matinee theatre mostly empty half-lit while the advertisements play, the Celebrity Guess Who questions and answers roll down the screen, the video clips of artists, musicians, singer-song writers, individuals.

A group of teenagers from the high school close by mull around the bottom of the theatre stairs trying to decide committee-style where to sit. The girls and boys alike, long Goth black hair over their gleaming eyes, dark clothing wrapped imperviously around their young bodies like swaddled newborns. So precisely, darkly put together that I don't know how they manage to dress each morning. I lean forward to take a closer look. No seams that I can see, as if they don't strip off the layer upon layer of black clothing at night, preferring instead to sleep in the dark, familiar fabric of themselves.

Rising early in the morning to re-apply the black Kohl around their eyes, straight-iron their shimmery black hair, apply the charcoal lips of their Goth-ness, so that when they are ready, darkly secure in their individual clothing, then they go

out into the dicey world—alone at first, their earned independ-
ent, tempting fate perhaps?

Then finding safety in their numbers—pioneers onto
themselves.

Protected, I pray, from the hard edge of razors, the steel
round of aluminum baseball bats.

The Goth group passes us noisily, oblivious to the in-awe
stares of Caleb and his friends.

"Look, mom," Caleb whispers, like they are foreigners in
his familiar land.

"I see," I say.

Caleb watches them pass.

"Cool," says Caleb.

The Goths sit in a line eight strong at the top of the theatre.
Caleb and his friends keep glancing back until one of them
says *Take a picture, it lasts longer.* Then Caleb and his buddies
break into titters of schoolboy laughter in the dark. We hear
the Goths laugh, too. Caleb glances up once more, one of the
Goth girls purses her charcoal lips at him in a pretend kiss, then
grins wide, shows the ordinary white of her adolescent teeth. I
glance down at Caleb beside me in the half dark, his small eager
face, the line of friends securely on either side of him waiting
for the movie to start—waiting for the yet-to-begin potential
of each other, the independence of themselves yet-to-be.

Caleb looks up, watches me tentatively in the dark, waiting
perhaps for me to release him; the blue veins pulse beneath his
colorless skin. I study his sweet, vulnerable face, see in his olive eyes
the depths that say *I'm ready, I'm ready, I'm ready, ready, ready.*

I breathe the black theatre air in and in and into my lungs
until they are full, hold it as long as I can. I exhale. My underwater fear released.

## Pioneer

I circle Caleb in my arms; feel the furnace of his heat, the fierce of his safety in mothers, numbers, he and me. It's all we have. We watch the individual blur of stills, the combined moving colours, the seemingly seamless images on the screen ready for the movie to begin.

## The Night Doors 1987

In the late evening after the regular hours we had to go in through the side entrance, the night doors. The nurse on the late shift called, said we should come, my mother, my brother and I. We came in a great hurry.

I drove in my father's small, white, fast car. My brother Joe was in the back. We used to joke with him, calling him Joe-One-Brow as if he were First Nations, though we were French-Canadian but he had the black thick hair of an Italian. His brow grew heavy and dark across his forehead. Sometimes when he was worried it looked like one long brow. Joe-One-Brow my mother would say, soothing her hand across his broad forehead when he still let her. Joe sat in the back of the car, my mother in the front seat smoking her long, thin cigarettes, looking out the passenger window. There were no jokes tonight.

I stopped alongside the white-rounded curb marked Loading Zone. The main entrance of the building was dark, the automatic doors shut. We had to go in through the side doors, so I pulled ahead. Joe and my mother got out and stood in the black foyer while I parked the car. I could see the single red ember of my mother's cigarette going from her face to Joe's and back again. My brother Joe did not smoke much but when he did, he did not buy his own.

We walked through the main foyer to where the elevators were, past the two rotund businessman statues that loomed dark and large before us, then the tall bronze sculpture that caught the pure light from the moon above. We went past the paintings, large charcoal drawings, the ceramic landscape that hung in triptych on the wall. So many pieces of art that people had donated to the clinic, some of it very good. Good, honest art, better than what you see in a gallery downtown. It made you feel all right about coming here to the clinic, and when I came during the day I never got tired of stopping to look at my favourite pieces even though we came frequently.

The night watchman was at his desk in the corner. He was a sizeable man with a big head and wide, soft shoulders that slid down from his neck, which made his grey uniform look the wrong size, as if it were not adequate enough to house him. He sat behind the desk with a magazine resting on his knee, and he looked up at us as we walked quietly past. We didn't look at him, only at the floor, freshly cleaned and polished. The smell of wax covered over the smell of hospital that assaulted your nostrils and made them flare when you first entered the building: the smell of soap and disinfectant, the warm stale air that circulated up from the floor vents.

The fifth floor corridor had been dimmed for the night, lit instead by small running lights along the black baseboards. The nurses in their white uniforms were gathered around a circular desk speaking to one another. One laughed out loud. They stopped talking while we passed, nodding their sharp white hats at us, their faces looking at once solemn, serious.

One room, ahead and on the right had a light coming from it. Not the overhead fluorescent but another kind, more yellow than the stark white, and Joe and I knew even before we reached the name-placard on the side of the door—it was my father's room. My mother went in first, we filed in behind.

Marie, my father's sister, was seated in a single foldout chair pulled up close to his bed. Her eyes were red. She was fidgeting with a large white handkerchief, on it monogrammed in black-stitched letters *Bill,* my father's name.

Marie raised her head up. She was beautifully tall, long in body and face, though now she just seemed gaunt and tired in her bones. She looked at my mother whose face was dark, intent on my father who was lying on the white hospital bed. And perhaps because Marie had been there all along, seeing him, she got up quickly and caught my mother by the shoulders to ease her. My mother did not stop, instead she moved around the side of the bed. The two women stood over the small bed, Joe and I held back at the foot of it so all we could see was Marie's tired face watching our mother closely. We couldn't see my father from where we were.

My mother drew a sharp breath and held it a moment; when it came out she was crying. Marie's face changed and broke. Joe and I moved around the bed as one, as if we did not want to be separated, and then we saw him, too.

My dad wasn't a big man. He was of normal height, maybe slightly less now because of the sickness but his bones were fine and smooth, small like a woman's but in a man's way. His eyes were dark, dark brown, you could never quite see your way through to what was underneath. His hair was cropped close in a brush cut, still thick and soft, and he was lying on his back so that his face and arms and legs showed no colour against the pallid blue of his hospital gown; his limbs and face grey like stone. His mouth hung open and dark, gaping on his clavicle bone. Some black whiskers in sparse patches on his chin.

And his breathing was funny, exaggerated, as if the air were thick and hurt his lungs. When he drew the air in, his whole body, even his hands and elbows and feet convulsed. Then nothing. His chest was quiet, waiting. We waited, also. The time seemed long before we heard a strange clicking noise that came from his throat and caught in the dim silence of the room. When he exhaled it came out loud and coarse, a terrible noise.

The nurses had raised the stainless-steel railings around his bed. The room was semi-private with only one other bed but there was no need to pull the linen curtains around his bed because there was no one in the other bed to be disturbed by the sight of my father. There had been a man. A man much older than my father, who, every time we came, was lying with his back propped forward facing the television from which you could not hear the sound. The man had clear tubes running out through his nose and mouth, tubes going in one arm, black with the red fresh blood. He always nodded his hairless head our way when we entered the room, and we asked him once if he'd like some of the cookies my mother had made. He smiled and shook his head, no. He did not speak. He never spoke. I thought perhaps it was because of the tubes, though I think he preferred the silence the same way he watched television.

Yesterday when we came, my dad wasn't awake anymore or talking nonsense because of the morphine about the thick-coloured ribbons that hung in the air before his face—he kept trying to stab them with his yellow wood pencil. Then the nurses came and moved the silent man in the other bed out.

The curtains were gathered on one side by a silver chain. The four of us stood by my dad's bed with the silver railings erected around him, us watching him as if he were in a cage. No one touched him. We were afraid to. His face remained granite and grey, untouched even by the violent convulsions, and that seemed absurd, that his face did not alter or show any of the pain when the rest of his body went crazy with the twitching, almost as if his head was not aware of what his body was doing. I hoped it wasn't.

As I stood watching my father, I felt the anger rise in me. The same anger, an anger without form or reason that I'd had when my cat caught a towhee last winter and brought it to me on the porch deck, the bird small and shuddering, still alive, twitching about like it was mechanical, not live. I killed it with the yellow straw broom I had in my hands and pushed it off the deck onto the hard white snow below. My cat went down after it and carried it in her mouth into the bare-thorned bushes of the blackberries. Later I felt bad, I didn't know if I was cruel or kind. I still don't know.

I felt the same way watching my dad on the hospital bed with his entire body, except for his face, shaking and shuddering like the towhee. I didn't know if he was in pain or not. I saw the flattened pillows beneath his head and I wanted to pick one up and press it over his face to make him stop. I wanted him to die neatly, fast, without his thin legs twitching or his chest heaving and gasping, without the violent spasms that made his fine-boned hands ball up into terrible whitened fists. Without everything that made it seem so horrid, so ugly, and at the same time made his stone face not know. Without my mother, my brother, Marie and I having to watch.

"How long has he been like this?" I asked Marie quietly.

She said he'd started just after she'd arrived—at ten. The time was five past twelve.

"Have you been here alone all this time?" Joe asked her.

Marie did not speak, she only nodded.

It was hard seeing him like this, seeing anyone like this, only worse if you loved him. It is slow and painful, not anything you'd expect. I don't know if everyone or every living thing dies this way. I've never seen anyone else in real life die before. Only the towhee and the rows of red snapper fish laid out on the docks after the boats had come in for the day, the fish with the flaming orange gills blazing in the last sun, seizing and choking on the earth air. They all looked the same. Even my dad. They all took so long, too. Not fast and quick and easy like in an old western on television. There is no dignity or respect or pride or any of those things you see in a movie or read in a book where someone dies and it seems majestic, romantic. It isn't. It isn't any of those things. Not anything you think a human death should be—only an animal fighting not to die.

A nurse entered the room. Joe asked her if there was anything she could do.

"This is only the beginning," she said. "There is not much we can do for him. He is unconscious, and we really don't know what he can feel, if he feels anything at all. He has a while yet, maybe a few hours in this way. Later he will change and you will know it is time by the sound of his breathing."

The nurse was silent watching my father on the bed. I thought it sounded as if she was talking about a woman giving birth—not someone dying. Later I thought there was not much difference between the two—the coming and leaving of this life are equally as harsh, equally as unknown.

Marie and I left the room and walked down the corridor to the lounge where a 'No Smoking' sign was posted but we smoked anyway.

"Are you all right?" I asked her.

"It is a terrible thing," she announced into the dark. She had my hand and was smoothing it in hers. I did not answer. We sat, smoking, the two of us looking down the corridor to where the softened yellow light was. After a while I got up to go back.

"I think I will stay here and rest for a bit," Marie said.

I could hear her blowing the smoke out into the dark air but I couldn't see it.

My mother was seated in the fold-out chair beside my father. My father's eyes were half shut and you could see the brown colour underneath. He looked as if he were drunk. His mouth stayed open like a dark gaping tunnel and made an abrupt click the way a metal catch sounds when you spring it open. You could hear the noise each time his chest inhaled the stale hospital air and made him convulse on the bed.

I looked at his legs. They were pale and bare except for the black ankle dress socks he always wore, even during the hot months with his leather sandals and denim shorts that were cut off crooked and frayed above his knees. And always they looked funny. The socks. Proper and funny. They looked funny here, too, in the clinic but in a sad way.

I glanced out into the hall. Joe was there, his face toward the wall. I walked out to him and put my hand on his back. He cried for a few moments more before he uncovered his face.

"There is nothing in this world that prepares you for that," he said, looking into the room. From the hall we could see my dad's black-stockinged feet twitching. The soft muted light in the room made it worse, out of context with the harsh reality of my father's convulsing feet.

We took turns through the night, Joe and I and Marie standing by his bed, or we sat with one another in the quiet non-smoking lounge, smoking our cigarettes in the blackness. A lamp sat on the table next to us but no one bothered to turn it on, much better to sit in the dark and look out over the city and the lights, and off in the distance, the darkened flat span of the prairie.

My mother remained in the room cradling my father's hand next to her face. She waved it in the air when she was afraid his breath took too long to come. It was a long, slow process but I could watch him now without the anger. Nor did I feel the pain his face did not show.

The rest of the patients were quiet in their rooms. The ones whose doors were ajar breathed slow and shallow as though they were asleep but I thought they could hear us going up and down the corridor and that they lay awake in their beds waiting, listening for the death.

"It is a hard thing for your mother to see him this way," Marie said in the unlit lounge. Neither Joe nor I answered.

"I mean because he is her husband. I don't know if it's the same if he's only your father or your son or your brother—but a husband." She broke off, and then she was silent, also. Soon she was crying for her brother. It didn't matter what he was, it was all the same.

As Joe and I walked down the hall, Joe took my hand.

"It's awful, isn't it?" I said. He squeezed my hand tight and did not reply. Then in a whisper, "Do you think Dad is in there?"

We both glanced toward the eerie light ahead and were quiet a moment thinking about it.

"No," I said, "I think it's only his body now. I don't think he can feel it."

I thought this was what Joe meant. Joe looked at me, his face white.

"I don't hope he lives this time. I can't watch him with the pain anymore." Joe was quiet and crying.

"Is that horrid?" he asked.

"No," I said. "It would be better if he just died."

Joe squeezed my hand again.

"I don't think he's in there, either," Joe whispered as we entered the room. Through the doorway we saw our father's thin legs convulse.

"Christ, I hope he's not," I said.

▲

Our mother was seated where we'd left her beside the bed. She was crying close to my father's face and her tears made his forehead glisten in the yellow light but his face did not know that, either. She was saying things to him about how the drinking never really mattered or the fights and the arguments, that my father was a good man and everything was going to be all right. I listened to her and so did Joe and Marie and it was harder to hear the words she was saying to his cold grey face than it was to see the dying. Because it was too late, it didn't matter anymore.

"Anne, will you come out for a cigarette?" Marie asked our mother. My mother looked up when she heard Marie's voice; her face tired and awful.

In a small voice she said to Marie that she couldn't, she couldn't leave him.

"I don't want him to be alone, not now. He shouldn't have to be alone."

We were all quiet. I don't think any of us knew what to say, as though it was my mother who was more alone at that moment than anyone. It showed on her face. My mother looked at all of us around her and my father on the bed, and she put her head down on the steel railing and cried for a long while. We stood a long time before one of us raised her from the chair and she came with us.

## The Night Doors 1987

As we turned to leave the room, we heard a loud click. The same click as before only this time it broke loud and clean into the night. My father was different now. His breathing had changed.

It came so suddenly, without warning. We all stopped, and even before we knew what was going on, our mother did. She had been with him. She knew.

She ran back to his side. His face moved now, his mouth jerked open and shut, then open again, and his black-brown eyes came open, also, abruptly as if surprised. My mother tried to lift his torso from the bed but no one realized what she was doing until she cried out, "No Bill, no, let me hold you, oh God let me hold you one more time, Bill."

But she couldn't raise his body up from the bed because of the steel bar and because she was being too careful like she might break him in his thinness. She kept saying, "Please Bill, please let me hold you." Even though my dad wasn't stopping her.

Marie and I went around the other side of the bed and lifted him into her arms. There had been no breath since the click. We waited. We waited in the yellow light of the room; I hated the soft sourness of it. We waited for his breath to come.

Everyone was quiet and scared. My mother held my father's thin body to her chest, his pallid blue gown hung free and I could see the sores down his sides and back were red and inflamed from having been sick so long. Seventeen years so long. It made me ache inside.

His mouth hung open, stilled now by my mother's shoulder. His eyelids were drawn far back over his eyes; their colour stared blankly. We waited for the breath to come.

Then our father exhaled harshly, sudden and loud. It was frightening. The sound came again, that rasped click, only this time it was longer before he drew a great sucking breath, long, the way you breathe when you're about to dive underwater. The silence followed. We waited again.

I held my breath with him. I think we all did because I could hear nothing in the room or from out in the corridor except for the black quiet. We waited for him to exhale into the silence, the three of us about the bed, my mother on the bed with my father small in her arms like a child, and everything in the world that mattered at that moment was in this room, in my mother's arms. We waited. It seemed a hundred hours went by.

No one spoke or cried or breathed but when I couldn't hold my breath any longer, it came out loud and sounded like a bleak sigh of relief. Only my dad's didn't.

I looked at my mother. I think, really, we all did because of what Marie said about her having the most to lose. Or perhaps because she was still waiting for my dad to breathe again when the rest of us knew and had stopped. My mother still waited.

Joe cried out or maybe it was Marie, hard to tell who, for the small room filled with the noise of shock, disbelief, crying. My mother must have realized then that my father wasn't going to breathe out. She shook him in her arms a few times as if she was trying to shake the air back out of him.

"Bill, Bill, Bill," she said shaking him, then she stopped suddenly, catching herself perhaps, and a look of terror spread on her face. She lowered him down on the bed; his head fell back first, heavily onto the flat white pillows. She got up from her chair; had to steady herself with one hand on the steel railing, she rose so quickly. She could not look at him now that the air did not go in and out of his chest. She was crying hard and turned from the bed almost in a run only she wasn't able to because her legs were too shaky. We could hear her crying loudly, and the nurses must have heard her also from the opposite end of the hall because soon after the weeping faded, and I knew my mother was in the elevator going down, going away, away from the room and my dad and the death; then the nurses entered the room.

Marie was concerned about his eyes, her brother's eyes. They were wide open, disbelieving. She couldn't get them to stay shut and asked the nurse if she had any pennies. I don't know where she got that, from the television perhaps. And I don't know if Marie was bothered by the sight of it or if she thought we were. Perhaps she thought my dad would have minded lying curled on his side, his head fallen toward his drawn-up knees, his fine bare hands sticking out beneath the steel rails like a still caged animal, his eyes dark, staring out at nothing or everything.

I went over beside Marie and put my hands on hers. They were cold and rigid on both eyelids. She looked at me, bewildered, as if she wasn't sure who I was. I told her it was all right to let them go.

"Is it all right?" she said.

"Yes, Marie, it's all right. It doesn't matter anymore."

"Then you think it's all right. You think? You think it's okay?" Marie withdrew her hands as though they'd been on something hot, like she expected the lids to spring open. But instead they opened slowly, casually, the way you open your eyes after a long, restful sleep, his short, restless life. We could see the dark, dead stare again.

Marie backed away from the bed and stood, water running down her face and long neck, streaking her cheeks crimson, no sound, her hands in fists against her temples.

Joe had been standing on the other side of my father. He was looking down at him saying some things I couldn't hear, smoothing his palm over our dad's thick black brushcut the way we used to when we were kids and my father was young, healthy, full and large with the world. It always felt like soft black grass. Joe looked up and asked if he could say a prayer, and someone, the nurse perhaps, said of course. It was a child's prayer, the same one we said as kids at night before we went to sleep, and it sounded odd for my brother to be saying it now. It wasn't until he got to the part "Now I lay me down to sleep, I pray the Lord my soul to keep, and if I die before I wake—" then Joe's voice cracked, faded into his tears. He barely whispered the "I pray the Lord my soul to take."

I don't know why but it made me sad to hear it again after all this time, and I felt like crying for Joe. I don't think I believed it anymore.

"I love you so much, dad." Joe put his cheek next to our father's. My dad's face grey in comparison. Joe stroked my father's forehead for a long time before leaving his side, reminiscent of my mother perhaps, or comfort for my father, though I thought it was for Joe. Marie went out with him. They were holding one another around the waist, and Marie stopped to squeeze my arm as they passed. She tried to smile for me.

"It's all right, Marie," I said. They left.

The nurses had turned the overhead fluorescent lights on. The lights were bright and white like the day and made the room appear bigger, more real now. I looked at the nurses and was surprised to see they had tears, also, running down their cheeks. I suppose I thought they'd seen this so many times before that they wouldn't feel it anymore. I thought it was something you grew hard to, though I think the tears were more for us, who were still here, acutely, painfully alive in this awful moment, than they were for my father who was neither in pain nor in this moment. I did not cry. I only stood by him looking at his knees that were round and thin, sharp with the bones underneath, pressed up towards his quiet chest.

The yellow pencils my mother had brought from his office along with the business files that lay untouched were on the table next to him. He hadn't felt like looking at the files, but he held the sharpened pencil in both hands the past three days even while he slept. Sometimes stabbing the coloured ribbons of light he said were there in the air that no one else could see. I'd tried to loosen the pencil from his grasp while he slept but he woke, clucking his tongue behind his teeth; he held it very tight.

"Will you take his things now?" one of the nurses asked. "Or do you want to come back for them tomorrow?"

I said I would take them now. I stood by the bed waiting while the nurses gathered his old terrycloth robe and clothes and brown felt slippers from the narrow closet, his shaving things and black-bristled brush from around the white en-amelled sink. They took his business files and put them into his Lufthansa Airline bag that he'd come in with as if he were ready to fly somewhere. I picked up the yellow pencil and held it tight while the nurses went about their duties cleaning the room, disinfecting and tidying, preparing for the next patient. None of them made a move to rearrange my father's body or do anything that way while I remained in the room. They worked their way around him and me till it became evident that the only thing left to do was him.

"What will you do with his body?" I asked the small, dark-skinned nurse next to me. She watched me with eyes so dark they were all one intense colour. She told me kindly, carefully that they would bathe him.

"And then?"

Then they would call the orderlies to come and take him away.

"To the morgue?"

"Yes, to the morgue."

I asked if the morgue were here in the clinic but the small dark nurse said no, it was farther along on the other side of the hospital. I didn't ask any more questions. I could not think about my dad lying on some metal sheet in a long drawer somewhere dark and probably damp, where there was no art, no paintings or clay sculptures, or the businessmen statues I liked. I would have felt better if his body could be here in the clinic among the art.

A tall nurse put her hands on my shoulders and told me his bag was ready.

"You can stay as long as you like," she said.

The nurses started to leave the room but the small, dark nurse stood a while beside me with her arm tight and comforting around my waist. She asked me if I'd be all right? I said yes and asked if I could say goodbye to my father. I felt confused, as if he wasn't my dad anymore, and the large kindness of the small nurse made me want to cry. But I didn't. She left the room.

I was alone with him now and I didn't know how to feel. It did not feel at all the way I thought it would. I didn't feel bad, really; I was glad he was dead. It was over but still it felt wrong.

I stood in the room with the fluorescent lights overhead. I saw on his wrists the holes where the tubes had been. The room was silent. The others had gone, and the brown Lufthansa bag was at my feet waiting for me. The yellow pencil was in my hand reminding me of my dad, my real dad, not the body on the bed waiting for the orderlies to come and take it away.

## The Night Doors 1987

I realized then what the matter was, why I was still there—what it was I was waiting for. It was his body. It wasn't some unfinished business you left for someone else to do. It was my father's body. It did not seem right to leave it here so small and white and helpless. This was when the tears came hot and burning down my face, and I could not stop them. Leaving him here seemed like the hardest thing in the world to do, as if I was leaving behind something terribly precious. I did not know what to do. I stood beside him, the tears scalding my face.

It seemed his thinness was in my arms, not heavy weight but light like a child's, and I was going down the corridor with the soft running lights along the black baseboards past the Nurses' Unit. The large circular desk was empty because they were looking for the orderlies. I stood at the elevator. My dad's eyes open and dull and staring. We went down. The doors parted onto the main foyer where we walked past the paintings and the two rotund businessmen statues, tall and looming, larger than us both. Along to the side entrance because it was night, late night. The big night watchman was at his desk with his magazine on his lap, and he looked up at me with my father in my arms. My father's pale-blue hospital gown hung over his thighs where the bones were loose and shifted while I walked. The night watchman did not say anything.

I saw the cars outside in the dark cold air. White exhaust ran from behind each car and hung stiffly in the night air. I walked to the first car. My mother was not there. I went to the second one, my father's small, white, fast car. She was in the front seat, smoking. They were all smoking, my mother, my brother and Marie till they saw me with dad's dead child-body in my arms standing next to the passenger window. It was bitter cold. I saw my mother's face; how it would break into the terror again. I knew I couldn't.

I knew I couldn't, as I stood before his body curled and quiet on the white hospital bed. I knew I couldn't as I touched my warm lips to his cooling forehead, his skin going white with the lights. My tears fell on his face and glistened on his cheeks. I didn't wipe them away. I said goodbye and picked up his brown Lufthansa bag and left the room.

I walked down the corridor with the dimmed lights along the black baseboards, and the rooms I passed were dark and the people in them breathed like they were asleep. The nurses were at the large circular desk in their white uniforms and soft-soled shoes. The orderlies were there, also. I heard them go quietly down the corridor while I waited for the elevator to come up from the second floor.

I got on in silence. The nurses watched me go. I walked through the main foyer past the paintings, the businessmen statues, past the main entrance, past the night watchman who was not at his desk.

Instead he was by the doors looking out at the two cars that were waiting, running in the dark, the white exhaust hanging like a dormant useless cloud in the cold stiff air. He was a big man and looked down at me. The tears wouldn't stop on my face. And he must have seen the brown Lufthansa Airline bag with the files sticking out, and the yellow pencil in my hand. I held it very tight. He knew. He didn't say anything. I felt his large hand on my back as I went out through the night doors.

## Tourist Girls

"The bikini contest says anyone over nineteen can enter," Marcy points out on the hand-scrawled poster. We flash our black mascara-ed eyes across the wood bar at the beerman. He lets his Jet Ski eyes glide over every watery inch of our bodies, especially Too-tall Marcy's, a former teen model for the Sears mail-order catalogue.

"We're at the quarter finals, girls," the beerman says, noting my paltry breasts; he looks like he could go south on us.

"We came all the way from Calgary," Marcy says.

I can almost see his spring-moose deliberation in the un-conditioned air above the bar as he surveys Marcy's pretty body once again; and she lets him. Then we all glance towards the comely lake out the large window; the town's frontyard, backyard, their every aqueous whim and playground. Despite the backwater current in the bar, the choking reek of coconut emigrating from the beerman's shaved head that wafts through the hot, dank room. The pristine lake out front with the blackfly smatters of motor/speed/power boats throbbing, pulsing, vibrating, an entire circling suburb of searching-for-fun houseboats atop the turquoise water. Puerile girls in string bikinis on boats, on ski ropes, on public display.

"Thank fact they are not nineteen," Marcy whispers to me in relation to the tweeners that the beerman is monitoring closely, likely his every aqueous whim. We monitor the V-man shape of the teenaged boys, playing beach volleyball that we wish were nineteen.

The stealthy way the perpetual wake sneaks up the blistering sand, cooling your toes, rhythmic-like on your sun-scorched skin, anesthetising your every skepticism—a personal ocean, really. We look back at the bartender.

"No tee-shirts, no buckets of cold water, no pig blood," Marcy states, more than inquires.

He smiles at Marcy, for her wit, we think, but then his swimming eyes pause, distracted, and we think less wit, more the wet-daydream he's having.

"A $400 diamond ring?" Marcy asks.

The beerman nods, flashes his tinfoil teeth at us.

The scene we envision: Us in our swimsuits on stage, tittering and laughing with the town girls while the judges look us over, then make their (no-doubt) quantified decision. Although the town girls may not laugh and titter when they find out the beerman let us tourist girls in at this late quarter-stage final. Nonetheless.

He pours a couple Bushwacker Browns. Sets up whisky boiler shots that Marcy knocks back, the cagey diamond player she is. Strong black smell from the brown water beer, I'm afraid of contracting Giardia like dogs. I sip on the whisky as disinfectant.

"So you mean we just stand in a line in our bathing suits with the other girls?" I ask.

"Something like that." The beerman snorts.

"I could do that in my sleep," Marcy says to me under her boozy breath.

"Wish you would, honey," says the beerman.

Marcy, unfazed, allows the corner of her soft mouth into a half-smirk. He looks at Marcy again, his loitering eyes, her well-proportioned breasts.

He lifts his chin at her, and me by default, motions with his unsheathed, lubricated head, tells us to *go on down, get ready, tourist girls.*

⚜

The quarterfinal girls are smoking cigarettes in the cement cellar next to the wood pallets stacked with the Bushwacker Browns, Station House Blondes and Talking Dog Wit from the local beer brewery in Salmon Arm. Too-tall Marcy has to duck under the low ceiling. The girls give us a once-over, searingly so, but we know they don't want to sleep with us, they only want to slot us in like that poker game, Higher or Lower? Lower, me, they decide after checking out my hundred-pound, meekly breasted body (is that muscle beneath her biceps, are those developed triceps?) They linger over Marcy's body, such the Sears Teen package she is; the heavy look on the town girls' faces says Higher.

Notwithstanding, the Hacky Sack thrasher girls are stiff competition. They are loose, agile, tanned in every orifice, definitely a lively playing field. Only the girl in the London Fog overcoat with the matching fedora and high heels will speak to us after the town girls turn away.

"You a body-builder?" she asks me.

"Amateur," I say.

"You girls have nice bodies," she says, not unkindly, sizing up Marcy.

She pulls her ivory belt tighter around her lean waist, no municipal sludge on her, either.

"What's with the coat?" Marcy asks.

"Like a private investigator," the girl tells us.

Marcy rolls her eyes at me.

"Like an act?" I ask.

"I want that diamond ring," the girl says, goes back across the low-lit room in her high heels.

Marcy lights a cigarette, we sit on a narrow bench. The soundman comes down later and asks us if we've chosen our music. The town girls titter and laugh, share a joint with the soundman, not us.

♟

We're lined up on the small stage behind a black curtain that the spotlight shines through the cigarette burn holes, which, if more evenly placed might seem mystical, transcendent even. But the burns are arbitrary, an impulsive randomness that makes me think more West Coast Seed(y) than Eastern Enchantment; that in combination with the hooting, hollering, boisterous sea of drunk males demanding the show begin.

The beerman/Master-of-Ceremonies, holding back the curtains, *Parting the waters*, he announces as he inspects the line-up of town and tourist girls (us) while we wait backstage for the soundman to queue up the music. The beerman's *Let's cut it up, girls* introduction that makes the crowd of intoxicated males roar, the town girls laugh, Marcy smirks, my exposed skin ripples.

Then the Red Hot Chili Peppers *Give it away, give it away now* from six-foot Sonic speakers. The yellow blare of the naked spotlight, the town girls parade out one-by-one, bikini-clad, alone on the stage amid the wolf whistles and ya babies and rutting grunts. When the girls come off stage, their half-mast eyes are shiny, faces aroused, limbs sweaty.

Ahead of me, London Fog girl adjusts her fedora, fidgets with her belt. The cheers, the whistles, the applause determining the Higher or Lower rating from one girl to the next is an unrestrained wave of white water noise. We can't discern one from the other. London Fog goes out. We catch glimpses of her through the burn holes. How she twirls her belt, coyly adjusts the slant of her fedora, winningly looks out over the ocean of stirred males as if in search of a partner, or better yet, multiples. Then the bass drops into dubstep, heavy, rhythmic, we feel the pulse in our own groins—it's London Fog no more, nothing but her tanned, brazen skin, thonged bikini. She can do the splits. Her hips-don't-lie gyrating to a skanky beat we're not familiar with. She gets a standing 'Oh' and thunderous applause that we're pretty sure means High Higher Highest.

"Gonna have to step up our game," Marcy breathes into my ear.

"From the city of Calgary, a professional body-builder," the beerman bellows.

Amateur, I want to say. Then the slow, sultry intro of David Bowie's *Putting Out The Fire*. I walk barefoot out onto the plywood stage in my leopard-skin bikini. The yellow spotlight assaults my eyes, renders me blind, the narrow runway that leads, horrifyingly it seems, into the gesturing arms and fingers and tongues of the lake-drenched males, the V-man teenaged boys (questionably nineteen) pressed up against the stage. The yeasty stench of Bushwacker and Talking Dog sans Marcy's Wit, the fermented guy heat in the pulsing, darkened room.

I can hardly stand the mandatory six seconds at the end of the stage. Every guy's eyes on my amateur body—their every aqueous dream and skin playground. The trucker with the ponytail beard that wants to do me, the shooter group at the bar mock-thrusting their pelvises in time to Bowie's chorus *putting out the fire with gas-o-liiiiiine.*

My boiler-shot stomach roils. I sprint back upstage, which prompts an encore mantra from the teenaged boys, and I'm forced to walk the wood plank once more.

Regardless, the rowdy applause, (high, though not London Fog high) from the non-discerning males, my backstage humiliation.

"Well, you sucked," says Marcy to me, her turquoise eyes flashing.

And suddenly I'm torn between my own shame, London Fog and Marcy In The Sky With Diamonds. *Tangerine trees, marmalade skies, the girl with kaleidoscope eyes.* Marcy bursts through the curtains, shifts her Sears catalogue shoulders back in her black rayon bikini, skillfully thrusts out her stunning breasts—an audible gasp from the Ever-Ready males. John Lennon in the air, psychedelic Lucy in the sky, Marcy struts the length of the plywood runway like she's in Milan and not some slant-water, backside lake bar. Her shoulder-length red hair, the long, cool drink of her Too-tall body, the swing of her professional teen hips, her parting-waters, her full, bursting lips. Giving it away on her own terms, which is what I adore about Marcy. The guys go wild chanting her name, like a moving, pulsing, ceaseless wake in the wet air. And secretly, beneath the West Coast Seed, the Eastern Disenchantment, the skanky beat I now know, I chant along with them *Marcy Marcy Marcy.*

## 7 Ways to Sunday

Miles sits on the front steps, lights an Export 'Eh'. Thoroughly Canadian, he is. The same two Jehovah's Witnesses who stopped in last week are coming up his walk in their buttoned-down shirts and ties. They remind him of Sharoma, who he works with at the Co-operative. She's Jehovah's Witness, too, but hot, like the Scotch bonnet peppers that he cons the teenaged kids in the produce department into tasting. Those peppers burn deep down in the back of your neck and just when you think you can't take it anymore, the burn subsides into a stay of execution and you know you've come through the fire, literally—a rite of passage that Miles finds hysterically funny.

He butts his cigarette out in Mern's potted chrysanthemums on the front step, which are badly in need of water, his wife having gotten up hours earlier this morning to catch the bus to Chapters where she works.

"Brother K," Miles says, nods his head at the other brother whose name he doesn't know.

"You guys an American outfit?" Miles asks the two young men. The acne-scarred one—Brother Kevin—says they have a head office in Pennsylvania.

Miles looks up at Brother Kevin and his comrade, who doesn't speak. Miles wonders if the guy is deaf, a mute perhaps, but he doesn't think so because he hasn't seen a pocketful of pens for sale beneath the guy's suit jacket. The pair of Jehovah's stand in front of Miles on his front step, ready to serve.

"Hey, do you guys know Sharoma?" says Miles. He doesn't know her last name.

Brother Kevin thinks he might know Sharoma, but when Miles describes her body part by body part, his fleshy face animated, his pale green irises ablaze, Brother Kevin says they probably aren't thinking of the same person. The Mute stares down at his black dress shoes.

"So what's on for today?" Miles asks. Glances sideways into the neighbour's yard where the single mother in a white halter-top is filling up her Beauty and the Beast swimming pool with the garden hose for seven squealing kids. She runs a daycare but the majority of the kids are hers. Miles thinks to tell Brother Kevin that he and his wife Mern, only have one daughter, Joleanne.

"Mern was seventeen when she had Joleanne and after that she couldn't have anymore. Tubal pregnancies. Nothing to do with me," Miles says. "My bullets are gold."

Brother Kevin nods, the Mute smiles shyly.

"Gold is one thing, but these people that go out and pro-liferate the already-overcrowded earth with eight, ten, a dozen offspring, well, that's just negligent," Miles says.

The two young men look at him uncomprehendingly.

"Mern's not a believer," he tells the Jehovah's.

He's not entirely convinced of the existence of God himself but he's willing, god knows he's willing.

"Perhaps we should come back next week and speak to your wife?" Brother Kevin asks.

"Knock yourself out," Miles says.

▲

Miles parks the racing bike he borrowed from three duplexes down in the rack at the front of the Co-operative store where he's working the late shift. He's early and has time for a cup of coffee and a cigarette so he goes to the break room. Sharoma, the Jehovah's Witness, walks into the break room; he wishes she would come over and speak to him with that gorgeous mouth of hers. In reality, he doesn't know what she's doing working in the grocery business, with those lips she could be personal assistant to some lucky, chunky-assed CEO of an oil company. Women like Sharoma don't stay long in this business. The work is too strenuous, the hours all over the place and the pay capped after a few years with no hope of moving up. Sharoma goes back to work. He looks around the break room and eyeballs the chirpy breasts on a group of young cashiers who ignore him.

He's big, he knows it. Probably carrying around too much weight for his 6'2" frame, but he's got a full head of red-dish-brown curly hair to make up for his size and he's riding to work now since the transmission fell out of Mern's Ford Taurus. Joleanne's boyfriend, the hundred-pound man, is taking mechanics this year and has it disassembled on their front driveway.

Miles finishes his third cigarette. He's got a rippling tide of nicotine going in his veins; feels like he's fuel-injected. For good measure, he pops a couple of pink pick-me-ups. Over-the-counter diet pills that he happened upon behind the pharmacy counter the other morning when he came in for his 5:00 a.m. shift. He hadn't realized how security minded the pharmacy was—all the locked cupboards and drawers. It would have been easier to break into the store safe than to grab a few samples of Ativan or Prozac, something nice and easy, to bring you floating down at the end of the day. Speaking of that, he should pick up some Nice'n Easy for Mern. Her hair is starting to go grey around the edges. She's only thirty-four. Christ, what's she going to look like when she's fifty-four? He washes the diet pills down with the last of his coffee. That should keep him until 10:00 p.m. He'll have to tell Mern she needs to take better care of herself. He doesn't really want to go out shopping for a new princess, but he is a man with standards.

He strolls into the produce department, stands around and shoots the shit with Richard, the full-timer and technically his boss, who is trimming romaine lettuce. Richard, like those automated voice prompts on the telephone, only responds to work-related questions.

"You're on tables tonight," Richard says. "Sharoma has the wet end."

Miles suppresses his toothy grin. He knows better than to take any shots where Sharoma is concerned. She's Richard's favourite and not because she's a *hot-looker* like the Asian work-study they hired once said.

"She a hot-looker," the Asian work-study said to Richard one day. He had to repeat it four times before Richard realized he was saying she's *a hard worker.*

Hard-working Sharoma goes by with a load of wrapped cabbage, rutabagas, snow-white parsnips. Miles pulls himself up and sucks his gut in.

"I want this place looking mint, Miles, I'm opening by myself tomorrow morning," Richard says.

Miles slaps Richard on the back and says no problem. They'll turn it upside down. Then he goes into the cooler and eats a dozen

$15.91/kilo Turkish dates. Out on the floor, the banana table is empty, save for a few discarded orphans that no one ever buys.

A customer comes over and complains to Richard. Richard puts down his lettuce and loads a cart, top to bottom, nine boxes high with Chiquita bananas and goes out to the floor. Miles comes out of the cooler, pulling a single box of Dole lemons across the floor.

"I've got it covered," he says to Richard and waves him off.

Richard disappears into the back. When he comes out fifteen minutes later, Richard's got his riding gear on and his fifteen-hundred-dollar mountain bike that never leaves his sight. It hangs from the rafters in the back room. Richard stops to give Sharoma a few last minute instructions. Miles watches him, wants to catch his eye and give him the thumbs up that everything is under control. He'll make sure Sharoma has the wet end spanking by the end of the night, or he'll spank her wet end, Miles thinks. Richard leaves the store without even looking in Miles's direction.

Miles finishes the bananas and goes over and tries to shoot something with Sharoma, not shit necessarily, anything really to get her talking so he can stare into her violet-coloured irises. But she must be related to Richard because the only thing she responds to is work.

"Well, I'm going for a break then, back in fifteen," Miles winks. The first of Miles's multiple breaks and the shortest may be forty-five minutes. Sharoma doesn't look him in the eye.

He runs into the good-looking store manager who veers off suddenly into customer service. Probably something important she's forgotten.

"Have a good one," Miles hollers after her. He'll catch up with her later.

By the end of the night, the wet end is spanking and so is Sharoma. Sharoma's face is glistening like a honey-dipped donut from her night's efforts. Miles would like to lick the fine layer of sweat off her exquisite puffy lips if she'd let him. When Miles first met Sharoma, he asked her if they were natural. Sharoma crossed her arms over her breasts. Miles laughed.

"Not those, hon, your lips. Are your lips natural?"

She walked away. Perhaps he could get Mern to go in for some collagen treatments. The thought sends a pleasant thrum down his spine.

"Good work," Miles says to Sharoma as she covers the potatoes with black plastic. "The tables don't look too bad either, eh?" he says.

Sharoma looks around the department. The only table that is full is the banana table stacked to the gunnels. By morning, the bottom layer will be black and bruised. She doesn't answer. Shyness, Miles thinks.

"You going to Boston Pizza tonight?" he asks.

He knows she never does. She has a husband, who is also Jehovah's Witness, who looks about thirteen years old. He couldn't get served even if he did drink. In between managing a Futon place and working construction part-time, the husband stops in occasionally to give Sharoma a ride home. Too bad Mern's Ford Taurus is out of commission; he could give Sharoma a ride home when the husband doesn't show up. Miles sees him sitting out front in a white shirt and neat tie. Miles wears his own tie like a parody of a drunk office worker—off-kilter and sloppily knotted. He wonders if her husband does the door-to-door thing. The husband drives an old Honda Civic. Miles thinks Sharoma deserves better: a better job, a better car, a husband that can take better care of her.

Then he remembers that Mern called earlier for him to pick up a specific piece for the wine maker and something else. What was it? Ketchup? He'd better hurry; the last till would be closing. He gets up to the front with the clear plastic spigot, a bottle of Heinz, a box of Nice'n Easy, Honey-Ass blonde like Sharoma's. He watches Sharoma climb into the small Honda Civic out front. The tills are closed. He stuffs the items into his knapsack. He'll catch up with them next time he works. His mind is only now starting to slow down to a steady hum after the diet pills. He might need a Corona to bring him down to ground floor. He digs into his pocket to see if he has any money and finds a twenty-dollar bill he didn't know he had. Bonus.

♠

He's talked the testicles off a few Jehovah's, and the odd vagina, too, but the latter are few and far between. They must save the women for the elderly, the lonely Oprah Winfrey-Dr. Phil-watching housewives and single mothers who run daycares. He's noticed the Jehovah's females tend to stop in next door and then skip a couple duplexes over where a pink-haired woman lives with five cats that look like some weird dwarfed variety of black panthers. The cats scare the crap out of Miles. They are large and muscular and unearthly feral for domesticated felines and black as the blackest African-American he's ever seen on *Cops*. The cats have intense yellow eyes that follow his every move when he saunters by to borrow the newspaper from the mailbox next to the pink-haired woman's.

The Jehovah's women rarely stop in at his place. Once, that he can recall. He remembers Sister Susanna—the older of the two, incredibly huge-breasted. He could hardly help himself from staring the whole time she was waving a copy of the

Watchtower in his face. He asked if her breasts were a liability in the god business? Sister Sarah let him have *The Watchtower* free of charge.

He sees them walk by now and then, and they do wave at him when he bellows out their names from his front steps:

"Oh Susanna! Sarah!"

The wave is hesitant, lacks the normal zeal of the Jehovah's Witness that Miles has become accustomed to from Brother Kevin and the Mute. It bothers him that he doesn't know the Mute's name, what with his uncanny ability to remember names and physical attributes. He's sure the Mute has never told him or Miles would remember it.

Mern's Ford Taurus is strewn out across their driveway that supposedly the hundred-pound man is going to put back together one of these days. He's not a bad kid; just doesn't have a whole lot going on upstairs and his life ambition falls, well, short; the kid wants to be a bloody mechanic. He has an unexplained scar down the centre of his nose that reeks of parental abuse and/or a knife fight. The last time Miles saw the hundred-pound man, he was sitting on a stump of wood on their driveway with a red-handled axe at his feet, a bowie knife in one hand, and a grease smeared carburetor in the other, looking more like he was out to murder something rather than fix it. By the time his daughter gets to second-year university, Miles gives the hundred-pound man 70/30 odds that he'll be blowing in the wind where she's concerned.

He lights a cigarette. Mern doesn't like him to smoke inside the duplex. Yellows the walls, she says, but Miles isn't concerned. They are renting until they can get a down payment together to build their own house. He'll put on an expansive wraparound balcony so he can enjoy his morning cup of coffee and Export

'Eh' on whatever side of the house necessitates his attention. As it is, he has to crane his neck far to the right to catch any view of the single mother in her backyard. Miles notices a swell beneath the single mother's breasts as he watches her overtop of his newspaper. He suspects she may be pregnant again.

He looks up and sees Brother Kevin and the Mute on the front walk. Jehovah! He'd talked so much the last time, he'd figured they wouldn't come back, but here they are.

"Good morning," Brother Kevin says, and waits for permission to approach. Miles nods at the two Jehovah's Witness to begin the approach. The Mute stumbles over the uneven squares on Miles' sidewalk.

Miles lowers his newspaper slowly. He doesn't want to appear overeager, but he's thrilled to have someone to talk to. The day can be long and laborious if all you have to do is worry about the endless stream of things that need to be done to keep a roof over your head, and keep his daughter, Joleanne, in the hundred and fifty-dollar pink DC runners that she wears, and his wife in honey-ass hair dye, if not collagen treatments for lips like Sharoma's. Frankly, he's glad for the distraction.

"My daughter won a math award for trigonometry," Miles tells Brother Kevin and the Mute.

"Not that you'd guess that by looking at either me or Mern." Miles shakes his head.

He didn't make it past grade nine and Mern narrowly made it through her last year of high school, which happened to be grade ten.

"I'm more the entrepreneur type," Miles says.

Neither Brother Kevin nor the Mute respond; they both have a four-year degree from bible college and Brother Kevin is working on a Masters in Economics.

His daughter wants to be a veterinarian.

"That's seventy G's a year or more." Miles beams up at them from the front step.

They smile down at him in their crisp, short-sleeved shirts standing on his rough-hewn sidewalk, their ties pressed and hanging perfectly vertical in the 30°-Celsius heat. The air is hot and still, and still, they're ready to shoot the non-existent breeze once more. They are a species unto their own with the patience of Job, Miles thinks, though he isn't sure if Job applies to their particular brand of god.

"Care for a coffee?" he asks Kevin, folding his newspaper over to the crossword puzzle. Both decline.

"Got a pen?" he asks the Mute.

♟

The television popped loudly and sent up a concluding coil of smoke just when Mern's *Cold Squad* was about to begin.

"Picture tube," Mern said. Though Miles didn't think modern televisions had picture tubes. That was last week.

Today Miles and the Mute struggle up the uneven walk carrying the monstrosity of a rosewood-encased television that Miles scored at the recycling depot. He talked the Mute into helping him transport the television home via the Mute's host family's borrowed pickup truck. Brother Kevin had a prior commitment, some seminar on money management. Miles suspected otherwise, a difference of opinion perhaps. He'd noticed over the past weeks, Brother Kevin becoming less eager, resistant, even, to Miles's world-view observations. Though they did agree on some things. Take marriage for instance: absolute solidarity as far as Miles was concerned, with which Brother Kevin concurred. Mern was Miles's soul mate. His cell-mate, he liked to joke, and normally Mern would find this funny also, but lately she seems to have misplaced her sense of humour; she rarely laughs anymore. And the man-of-the-house thing, *Glory be to thy father* appealed to him also: the husband, the father, the hunter provider. Yes, it's unfortunate that Mern is their Chapters meal ticket at present, but it's transitory, a matter of temporal circumstance, a short chapter in the larger book of their life.

By the time they get the television up the front steps and into the living room, both he and the Mute are sweating.

He wishes he knew the Mute's name: he hates to refer to him internally as the Mute, but at this point the impropriety of inquiring after so many visits was—well, Hell, it was like *not* breaking bread at Sunday dinner with a fellow believer. There is something sweetly preserved about the Mute that Miles likes; like that last, savoured jar of canned peaches that reminds him of his own sweet, silent daughter. There are things in this life beyond words, beyond god, Miles thinks, as he shakes hands with the Mute in gratitude for his help. Like the implicit love a father has for his daughter, the overt pride of a grade nine entrepreneur whose daughter wants to be a veterinarian.

♟

Miles plugs the television in and the image comes up slowly, the same way the first light of the morning is coarse and fuzzy when Miles opens one eye and sees Mern sitting on the edge of the bed. Her shoulders are slumped with sleep, a soundless complaint of too much weight, work, too early; too much in general, perhaps. He smoothes his palm across her back and then down over her broad buttocks, back and forth, back and forth, asks with a slow smile coming onto his face if he can help with anything. Mern doesn't answer.

She leaves the room and Miles hears the shower as he lies in bed. Miles wishes he could do more, but there are only so many hours in a day and running a house is hard work, too. He's the husband, the father, the holy provider—or at least he will be soon when he gets on full-time in produce. For now his sacrifice is that he's the man-about-the-house. An insult to his manhood, he knows, but he likens it to being married to a feminist, even though he knows Mern would rather die than light her brassiere on fire with a Bic lighter. Seventeen years of hard work and all Mern has to show for it is a slightly exotic papaya-coloured brassiere purchased from the Bay. No working car, no house, no vacation destination. Despite Mern's views on feminism, religion, her utter devotion to her in-menopause mother that she visits every Thursday without fail; Mern is a Promise Keeper's wife, a Jehovah's Witness dream, a true romantic, a Real Woman. Miles is enormously proud of Mern for her sacrifice.

♟

Miles saunters into the Co-operative twenty-three minutes late.

"I'd like to stay and chat," he says to Sharoma, who is working the floral section, but he can see Richard gesturing at his watch out of the corner of his eye. "Looks as if Richard is on the warpath again."

He rolls his eyes. Sharoma doesn't look up from what she's doing.

He wanders over to tell Richard the reason he was late is that Joleanne's teacher called just as he was going out the door.

"She seems unusually quiet and distracted lately," the teacher said. "She's normally so focused. She got a C minus on her trigonometry test the other day."

Was there anything happening at home? Anything the teacher needed to be aware of? Miles didn't think so. Joleanne was always abnormally quiet in his mind and as for the C minus, who ever used trig in real life anyway, he asked the teacher. That's not the point, the teacher said; she's my best student.

"You got me," Miles said.

He never saw her or the hundred-pound man anymore. What kind of student was he, Miles asked? The teacher didn't answer. Certainly the money was tight and Miles wasn't getting too many shifts right now and they were a little behind on the rent. He hadn't seen Joleanne for a few days now or maybe it was last week. He was working nights and by the time he got home from B.P.'s, it was well past midnight. Feasibly, he couldn't expect anyone to be up at that hour, distracted daughter or not, except for Mern, of course, who would get up and throw a leftover plate of dinner in the microwave for him, then go back to bed as he showered the persistent smell of celery off his body. But no, as far as Joleanne was concerned—nothing unusual, nothing out of the ordinary.

"My guess is it's pure and simple puberty. You know how moody teenage girls get," Miles says to Richard.

Richard shakes his head, and says no, he doesn't know, his oldest daughter is four. What he does know is that if you can't show up for work on time, he's going to get moody, too. Richard walks away.

Miles surveys the wet end. He's happy to take over where Sharoma left off earlier in the day. It looks mint already. He won't have to do much to keep it up for the evening. He glances across the floor at her. She is a hard worker. She bends over to remove the brown buds off the chrysanthemums as Miles admires the athletics of her legs in her regulation black shorts.

He wonders if she's a runner. She waters the stand of gangly ferns with a metal watering can. The spout is not overly long but thick and more than adequate for the job, Miles notes. Then she moves over to the circular stands and shines the leaves of the rubber plants with such care that Miles feels his own spout (his freckled trout he calls it) lengthening in his XXL Mr. Leggs pants. He puts his hand in his pocket.

Miles nods at Richard, who is watching him closely from the salad section. Miles goes into the back room. Happy to get off the floor and stand in the cooler until his thickening trout subsides, he has a hankering for something to tide him over; the pink diet pills make his stomach rumble. He eats a few snow peas and peels a couple of tangerines, then finishes a MacIntosh in three bites but he wants something more. He leans against the stacked boxes of Sunkist lemons/limes/grape-fruit and strokes, strokes, strokes his penis beneath his Mr. Leggs, his breath short, rapid, then easy-squeezy, lemon-peezy, his desire done in a moment.

He adjusts his cooled-down trout in his pants, comes out of the produce cooler, opens up a box of salted cashews and fills his apron pocket. He opens a few other boxes: some assorted jujubes and sour peaches and chocolate-covered raisins, fills another pocket. He smoothes his hand over his belly, thinks he detects muscle beneath the dwindling layer of fat.

He can smell the cigarette smoke from the plywood make-shift lounge and decides to duck in for a quick one. The store manager smokes, too. He sits down across from her.

"Great weather we're having out there, isn't it, Evelyn?"

Everyone else calls her Ms. G, or ma'am. But Miles doesn't; he's trying to straddle the age-old problem of *us versus them* where management is concerned.

Miles doesn't know what the G stands for. Godiva or something, he guesses. She wears her auburn hair up all the time but
it's a massive mane that Miles suspects falls down around the
small of her longish back when let loose. Evelyn looks at Miles,
briefly, as if confused. Then she stubs her newly-lit cigarette out
in her coffee cup, which strikes Miles as strangely erotic, raw
with rough edges, stainless steel. She gets up. Miles watches her
walk out, her back end swaying like a slow beat metronome.

♟

Miles carries the polished rubber plant that he missed paying
for because by the time he'd finished cleaning the back room,
the tills were not only closed, but most of the staff had already
gone. He could see Evelyn up in Customer Service beginning
to balance the day's take. He walks out through the vacated
grocery warehouse stopping along the way to light an Export
'Eh'. He blows the smoke out into the dark. He rummages
through the hardware shelves for the discarded bungee cords
he spotted earlier when he was helping a customer find some
door hinges that were out-of stock on the floor.

Outside the warehouse door, he straps the rubber plant
sideways onto the back of his bicycle. He'll skip B.P.'s tonight,
mostly because he thinks he can't handle the beer and the bike
and the plant. He wonders if there is such a thing as drunk riding. That strikes him funny and he laughs out loud in the black
night and flicks his cigarette butt into the cardboard compacter.
The sky is hazy, no stars to speak of, or gaze at, or wish upon.

The air is dry and warm. Astride his bike, Miles shifts his
body in his work clothing like a cyclist gearing up for the Tour
de France. He considers B.P.'s again but he's got an appetite on
him like a spring bear, amazingly in more ways than one. He

slides his fingers over the polished leaves of the rubber plant. He looks up at the obscured sky. Too bad about the stars, he's a man who truly appreciates what is in front of him. He detects the distant smell of smoke in the dry air, probably controlled burning in Banff, a fire in BC possibly. He lights another cigarette and wheels down the grocery ramp out into the hot night with his rubber plant strapped firmly in place.

♦

He wonders if Mern noticed the rubber plant on the television cabinet this morning. She didn't come back in and kiss him good-bye before she left for work like she usually does. He didn't bother to wake up even briefly this morning. He did himself in with last night's husband/wife conference. A tantric humdinger, if he thought so himself. Miles's trout stirs distractedly at the thought of Mern's sleepy face, her eyes closed in rapture as a result of his remarkable staying power. He suspects the diet pills may have something to do with it. Lucky for Mern that he has an endless supply. No one in pharmacy seems overly concerned about the behind-the-counter stuff.

Soon Mern will have a svelte husband, like the steady stream of guys Miles sees visiting the single mother next door. You'd think four children might be a deterrent, but that doesn't seem to stop them. Mind you, pregnant or not, the mother next door is young and has both her wit and shape about her. He wishes Mern weren't so worn-out all the time. These days she barely seems to notice him, as if he's become yet another chore that she has to attend to before she goes to bed early while Miles stays up and watches *Cold Squad* by himself.

He glances across the room at Joleanne's Grade Twelve (good god, where did the time go?) picture with her flat brown hair like plywood boards on either side her head, her meek, watered-down blue eyes staring out at the photographer, no smile on her thin lips. She's on academic honours at school but you wouldn't know it from looking at her picture.

He looks out the kitchen window and sees the single mother in her backyard, the mill of small, laughing children about the yard, the mother lounging in the Beauty and the Beast swimming pool, smoking a joint—something he's never been partial to, and frankly, doesn't consider it great role-modelling, either. Not to mention it's illegal in Canada. Two of her kids are out in the alley pitching rocks at the black panther cat on his back fence. He can hear the thud of stone on wood.

"Hey, cut that out, you little shits," he yells through the wrecked screen.

The mother looks at him vacantly.

♟

In the basement Miles finds a bottle of wine that he didn't know they had. It's white, not to his liking, but Mern will drink it and it will save him from spending the day bottling the batch of rosé that's ready. He can save that for tomorrow, or if it rains, if it ever does. It's been a dry, hot drought of a summer already. He wanders past Joleanne's bedroom and, from the vacant look of things, Joleanne has moved out and forgotten to tell them, at least Miles. Perhaps Mern knows? Mern didn't say anything after their session last night—come to think of it, she didn't say anything during it either. She must have been more exhausted than usual.

Mern lost an hour's sleep last night, but today, it appears, Miles has lost a daughter. Joleanne's downstairs bedroom—with the exception of her stripped-down Futon bed and crooked pine dresser that Miles needs to hammer back together properly—everything else is gone. Her clothes, her stereo, the fourteen-inch purple Visions television Miles got for her birthday last year because he knew someone who worked in the warehouse. The hundred-pound man's six-string guitar and pile of clothes that usually sit in the corner are also gone.

Miles sits on the naked futon and feels the void in his stomach beyond the dull rumbling of the diet pills. He looks around the barren room—it's as if his daughter never existed. How did this happen? When things were going along so smoothly, so according to his master plan, that once he got full-time work, then they'd all move into their own unattached house and buy a matching four-seater leather sofa and love seat. And all of them, including the hundred-pound man and Miles' mother-in-menopause-law, could sit together and watch *Top Cops* and talk during commercials.

Miles on the hard edge of a pine bed; he wishes he could call a time out, a rainy day to start over and take stock, take a little more time to plan things better. The house so still, so quiet, so lonely. He looks around the room, the bottle of white wine at his feet, then holds his woozy head in his hands.

♟

By the time the Jehovah's come, Miles is twelve sheets to the pisser on the front steps, and the air immobile with heat.

"Is that how that expression goes?" he asks Brother Kevin, who looks uneasy.

After finishing the bottle of white wine in Joleanne's VACANCY bedroom, Miles staggered back and forth, up and down the unfinished wood stairs, six times according to his count, filling up Mern's Pyrex measuring cup from which he's drinking. His measure: twelve cups, he tells the Mute. He holds up Mern's two-cupper, the rosé sloshing around the cup and a quarter mark. His face and neck are crimson from the sun.

"Perhaps we should go inside," Brother Kevin suggests.

"I can't," Miles says.

His daughter is gone and his wife will be upset. He covers his face with his hands and it looks as if he might cry, but then, through his hands, he says in a muffled voice that he needs to mow the back lawn and fix the picnic table and build a shelf in the living room for Mern and put the car back together again.

He raises his head up and looks over at the driveway and sees that Mern's Ford Taurus is not there.

"Holy shit," he says, and then apologizes to the Mute.

Brother Kevin can handle it, he thinks, but there is something susceptible about the Mute that Miles wishes to protect, like his daughter. She's too young to be on her own, and the Mute, too. She's not at all like him or Mern. The world will have her for breakfast. She's seventeen—she should be loud and have a pierced nose and spike her hair up into a rainbow Mohawk and wear gaudy red lipstick so that the world will damn well pay attention to her. Miles grows quiet and stares at the dark oil-stains on the driveway.

Brother Kevin and the Mute glance at the driveway. Indeed, there are no car parts to be found. Miles can't get over it, and the fact that his daughter is gone, not just gone so that all that he does see of her is the ghost of her flattened brown hair and pink nightgown disappearing into the bathroom every fourth morning or so, depending on if Miles has roused himself out of bed before noon or not. But now she is truly gone.

He points to the ex-vicinity of the Ford Taurus.

"Possibly your wife called a tow truck?" Brother Kevin asks.

Miles doesn't think so. He thinks the hundred-pound man somehow got his axe and his act together, and now he and his too-quiet daughter are headed somewhere far away from both him and Mern. In his mind's eye, Miles sees his daughter driving off in the Ford Taurus. He wants to wave, tell her to come back, he and Mern will try harder, but he can't muster the strength at the moment. They should have bought a sofa a long time ago. They should have turned the television off once in a while and talked to each other more than just during commercial breaks from *Cold Case, Top Cops*. They should have gone to church. They should have stripped down the back fence together. The family that works together stays together.

Conceivably, it was a mistake to let Mern work full-time at Chapters all these years, he tells the Jehovah's, who don't disagree with him. If Mern were at home like mothers were supposed to be, this might not have happened. Brother Kevin agrees that god supports the woman at home. He doesn't mention that god also supports the man at work looking out for his family. Miles tries to stand up, but god isn't supporting him and he falls heavily against the screen door. The screen rips through entirely and Miles is half on the front step and half in the house.

"Like my life," he says. "Halfway to nowhere."

He gestures wildly with his free arm. The Mute looks down at the ground. An enormous amount of affection fills Miles suddenly and if he could manage to stand up right now, he'd put his arm around the Mute, who is sombre and serious like his daughter, Joleanne. For god's sake let them have some fun in this life.

"God only grants you one fish," Miles slurs.

"Fish?" Brother Kevin asks.

"Life," Miles says.

"God only grants you one life?" Brother Kevin leans in for clarification.

"*Wisssh*," Miles says, making the word sound like a soft gust of wind.

He tries to focus his eyes, but the sun is bloody bright and he can hardly keep his eyelids open. The Mute shifts like he's suddenly ill at ease in his skin, like *his* soul is in need of rapid recovery. Miles unwraps one finger from around the Pyrex measuring cup and points up unsteadily at both of them.

"Live before you disappear into the forgetfulness that takes the place of your trout," Miles says.

Brother Kevin helps him to his feet. Miles takes one last sip of wine out of the measuring cup and tosses it into the half-dead juniper bush on the side of the duplex. The cup lands with a heavy thud. The Mute holds the ripped screen door open. Brother Kevin leads him into the house and arranges him in the canvas chair that Miles wishes were leather and a four-seater. The last thing Miles hears before he passes out into forgiveful-ness is the sound of someone's lawn mower starting up.

⚑

Sharoma has a black eye. From a baseball, she says, but Miles thinks it's the husband. He thinks Sharoma may have got-ten too far above her station as a woman for the Jehovah's Bastard. He'll have to go out one night and have a fist-to-eye conversation with Sharoma's husband. He notices Sharoma seems more passive lately, will actually stand around and lis-ten to Miles. Sharoma still doesn't look him in the eye, but

Miles figures it's something akin to shame for her black eye. No baseball did that.

Miles has his own problems. It's been five days now and his daughter hasn't surfaced. Mern has taken a few days off work from Chapters. Miles has been trying to pick up some extra shifts to cover for Mern and to mask the empty hole he feels in the pit of his everything. When Miles comes home after work, after B.P.'s, Mern is awake and sitting at the kitchen table with a plastic, long-stemmed wine glass the colour of citrus fruit. It makes the rosé wine inside look like panther piss.

They don't think anything horrible has happened to their daughter. Miles spoke to the hundred-pound man's mother. Apparently *his* father went out one day four years ago and hasn't come back yet.

"Please call us if you hear anything. Mern is beside herself," Miles says. He hangs up without waiting for the mother's goodbye.

Sharoma comes over and says she's taking her lunch break. She asks Miles if he would please watch the wet end for her. Miles is overcome with nostalgia for the days when he first started at the Co-operative and everyone was polite to him, understanding, co-operative even. He does his best to try to get to work on time. He does try to do a first-rate job, be a more-than-adequate guy. But down deep he knows he's a middling guy doing a run-of-the-mill job. At least that's what Richard wrote on his last employee evaluation. There's nothing wrong with that, is there? Slow and steady wins the race, doesn't it? Now is not the time to fly off and get hysterical. Someone needs to be Mern's rock of ages. He is all she's got left now. It's him, he knows, it's hymn.

Miles examines Sharoma's black eye. Life is no wish; it's strife and hardship and lacks fish. He'd like to reach out and stroke her face, cover his hand over her bruised eye and make the hurt leave from his stomach, from Mern's puffy eyes in the morning from too much crying the night before. He'd like to take the world and make it a place where breakfast is served to everyone regardless of how flat their hair, how watered down their eyes. That the meek shall inherit the earth is a myth perpetuated by a truculent god. He's no longer sure he wants a part in that. He wants his daughter back.

He looks at Sharoma, who is still standing in front of him, and says, of course, he will watch the wet end for her.

"Take some extra time," he says.

She turns and walks to the break room. After Sharoma leaves he busts his butt filling the broccoli and restacking the jumbled cabbages. He feels her pain. He goes through the bulk parsnips for the droopy ones that remind him of dogs with limp dicks. He tests the parsnips' worth by shaking them systematically in the air. He is there for her. He turns the five-pound bags of Bunny-brand carrots over in a uniform show of the cartoon bunny on the front. He is at one with black eyes. He re-trims the romaine lettuce and stacks them, like Richard does, in organized layers, something he's never done before. Then he goes through the red peppers one by one, setting them end-to-end in precision rows on the three-tiered shelf.

When Sharoma comes back she seems genuinely surprised. Miles has a fine line of sweat on his top lip. It's salty on his tongue. Sharoma almost touches him on the arm when she thanks him.

"No problem," Miles says, and he means it.

It feels good to put an 'A' student effort forth, instead of his usual grade nine drop-out attempt. He's a middling guy doing an outstanding job. He wishes Richard were here to see it. Miles goes into the back room and comes out with two fully loaded carts of Washington apples. He spends the next hour stacking American apples onto the Canadian tables, as high as they will go into the Egyptian flat-topped pyramids like they do at Safeway. He catches Sharoma glancing over at him, and waves hello across the floor. She waves back.

♟

Miles spots Richard coming into the store in his cycling clothes. He wonders what Richard is doing here; he doesn't work the dreaded night shift. Although Miles is glad, relieved almost to work nights, the more the better lately, if only to give him a break from the awful silence of his rented duplex, Mern's sad face that he can't fix, and his own ever-looping thoughts about his daughter, Joleanne, who has yet to resurface. He pushes the thoughts out of his mind. He's also glad to see Richard, because, for once, the department is full and clean and organized, and there's even long English cucumbers sliced up in the demo tray with Renee's Gourmet Dill Dip.

"What up?" he asks Richard.

Richard surveys the department.

"Sharoma work today?" he asks.

"No," Miles says.

Richard raises his eyebrows. Miles sees Evelyn G., the store manager, coming across the floor with a DVD in her hand. Miles stands taller and sucks his dwindling belly in. He's lost thirty-two pounds in the last month and some. He can see the archaeology of his cheekbones in the staffroom mirror.

"Working tonight, Evelyn?"

Evelyn bypasses him and walks into the back room to talk to Richard. Richard nods in Miles's direction once or twice, then Evelyn hightails it up to her office while Richard fusses around the back room spraying down the stainless steel counters and squeegee-ing them off. He comes out with the relatively new kid that Miles tested the Scotch bonnet peppers on and tells him to take over the department for Miles. The new kid nods his head; neither of them looks Miles in the eye.

"What's up?" Miles asks again formally, though he feels a hollow forming in his daughter-less pit along with Mern's puffy face.

"Meeting in Ms. Gorgon's office."

*Gorgon*? Miles is momentarily distracted. No wonder everyone calls her Ms. *G*. Gorgon sounds like some evil adversary on a kid's television show. Despite his heaviness, his hollow, he tries not to grin, but feels the corner of his mouth rise up into what must look like a smirk to Richard. Richard looks disgusted.

In the boardroom, Evelyn has a television set up. Miles nods at her. She doesn't nod back. The Stanley Cup play-offs have started and Miles hopes to some remote god that that's what the television is for.

"Hockey Fight in Canada tonight, Evelyn?"

Ms. Gorgon looks at him sharply. No one says anything.

Evelyn inserts the DVD he saw her carrying earlier and presses the play button on the remote.

"Training video?" Miles asks.

Neither Richard nor Evelyn answer.

"Sit, Miles," Evelyn says to him like a dog.

Miles sits at the other end of the oval table, nervous at the prospect of the DVD. Perhaps he's wrong. Perhaps it's the start of something positive; god knows he could use a little constructive activism in his life right now. Could be Richard wants to groom him for full-time work?

The DVD starts and Miles watches a shadowy figure hoist itself over the pharmacy counter. Miles thinks he recognizes the Mr. Leggs pants. Then someone, although Miles isn't completely convinced yet, due to the granular quality of the DVD, but the guy rummages through the unlocked cupboards behind the pharmacy counter and slides out a couple of flat boxes and puts them in his pants pocket. The video goes fuzzy for a few seconds, obviously an amateur production. The next frame shows the guy, yes, definitely the same guy, putting items into a backpack. Miles's slim, brief hope for constructive activism goes fully sideways.

Then a man, in the shadows of some cooler, could be dairy, deli, produce; Miles's sickened face knows which one. The man is leaning against a stack of boxes, stroking himself. Mrs. G. swivels forward in her leather chair to make out the brand names on the boxes that aren't decipherable. Miles refrains from telling her it's Sunkist. He looks down the long oval table at Richard, who is watching intently.

"Good god, stop," Miles whispers to himself.

Both of them look at him, neither respond.

Mercifully the shot cuts out before the shadowed man reaches his natural conclusion. No one in the room says anything, including Miles. He watches the next, same figure with his back to the camera filling his pockets with something from the Bulk Foods department. He shifts uncomfortably in his chair.

And then he sees himself, 6'2", plainly-lit, fully, recognizably in his XXL Mr. Leggs pants, wandering through the grocery warehouse with a huge rubber plant in his arms. Outside in the dark night, black and white now on the infra-red security cameras, he straps the plant onto the back of his borrowed racing bike with the bungee cords he found on the hardware shelves. The camera missed that. But the coup de grâce is the shot of Miles flicking his cigarette butt into the cardboard compacter bin and gliding out of the picture frame on the bike with the unpaid-for rubber plant strapped firmly in place.

The grand finale, the final nail in his pine coffin: the fire crew arrives, sirens roaring, red lights a spin in the dark. Miles spots Evelyn immediately in the DVD. She's got an overcoat pulled on over her pyjamas; he discerns a teddy of some kind beneath her coat, possibly crimson with black flimsy lace like the one he bought Mern. Evelyn's hair that is always up at work, is down and long and richly thick, and, as Miles suspected, hangs well past her small waist.

The verification of this realization is marred only by the closing shot on the DVD, which features, like evidence in an unwavering documentary, the cardboard compacter fully on fire with thirty-foot high, orange-reaching flames that light up the starless sky.

♠

Miles catches the tail end of his daughter's soft, deflated voice as he walks in the front door of his unlocked duplex. No reason to lock what he doesn't have. Mern is gone, his daughter is missing in action. He runs to the telephone, but too late. The voice message clicks off taking his daughter's sweet canned-peach voice with it. He stands at the kitchen window washing his celery-stained hands with Joy dish soap, gazes out at the single mother next door. The mother is chatting up some young guy while two of her four kids are scaling the back fence in an attempt to knock off another of the black panther cats. Miles notices that someone has trimmed the dead flowerbeds and mowed the patchy lawn, repaired the broken picnic table. Who, he wonders?

Miles pushes the button on the voice mail. Mern's voice comes on, more tender than he can remember it in years, repentant almost. It makes Miles want to sit down at the kitchen table and cry. He shuts the water off and listens carefully, though he's heard it six times already. She is over at her mother's and will likely spend the night as he is working late. She will see him tomorrow after she takes her mother down to Bay Day at Market Mall. *Tomorrow* was yesterday, and, like his daughter, Mern is not home yet.

Then Richard's voice comes on. His paycheck and record of employment will be ready by the week's end. Don't bother to come down, Richard says, we'll send them out by mail. There's no slouching where Richard is concerned. No sooner had Miles turned in his apron and emptied his pockets of salted cashews and Bridge Mix along with his employee swipe care and the seven box cutters he'd acquired from various places, and walked out of Evelyn Gorgon's office, than he sees the new kid already covering his tables. And here was Richard on his message machine before he'd even made it home on foot, the borrowed racing bike gone from the rack out front the store, most likely borrowed back.

Miles opens the fridge door and pokes around through the wine and the plastic squeeze bottles of Heinz ketchup. He arranges the ketchup bottles in a single line, neat, and accounted for. If he'd only understood the importance of piano lessons and gymnastics for his daughter, he might not be sitting an abandoned man in a deserted kitchen with no wife to heat the Saran-wrapped plate of steak and cheese potatoes from three days ago, for which Miles has no appetite. Instead, he pours himself a tumbler of wine in one of Mern's brightly coloured plastic glasses and sits down at the kitchen table for the last message.

He pushes the button on the machine. The one he wants to hear the most, the one he can hardly bear to hear. Joleanne's hesitant voice comes on. She's hesitant not because she's hurt or in danger (it comes out in a rushing sob near the end of the message) but because she's pregnant.

"Sorry, sorry, sorry," she says, melancholy on the message machine.

It turns out that it's not the 23-year-old single mother next door who is pregnant and going to pot in both mind and body, not the delinquent owner of four affection-starved kids with young lusty men dripping off her everything, but his 17-year-old daughter. His academic honour roll daughter. His veterinarian daughter. Miles puts his head in his freckled hands and exhales through his fingers. He can hear the metallic echo of Mern's voice in his wearied mind, telling her mother the same exact thing seventeen years prior. He didn't wish for it then, nor does he want it now, for his bright, hopeful daughter. His and Mern's hope riding in her watery eyes, despite her flattened brown hair. God, Miles thinks, not for her.

The phone message is long and winding and Miles is glad, despite his sore heart, to hear her small voice, the voice of a child really, his child, not the voice of a teenage mother expecting a child of her own. It reminds him of the time when Joleanne was five and she came running into the house to report to Mern that she *inadvertently* (her words exactly; Miles remembers the kindergarten teacher told them early on that they did indeed have a wonderfully gifted child, but sombre, too, and that could bring challenges) but Joleanne had inadvertently broken the handle off the shed door and she was sorry, sorry, sorry.

Well, he's sorry, too, unbearably sorrier after each glass of wine he consumes at the kitchen table while he replays his three messages four more times.

"Sorry, sorry, sorry," he says in unison with his daughter's voice on the message machine.

♟

The following day Miles doesn't bother with his daily ritual of getting out of bed. Rather he lines up the newly bottled rosé wine next to the bed as he finishes them. There is something about the green line of unlabeled bottles glinting like a glass moat in the afternoon sun around the perimeter of his bed that makes him feel less alone, more like a man with a mooring, a man with a secure anchor—a man with more.

♟

Day One Monday:
Three bottles of rosé drunk chug-a-lug style, prostrate on the bed. Seventeen phone calls to mother-in-menopause-law. Aim: Mern. Fruition: Busy tone.

Day Two Tuesday:
Miles looks out the bedroom window and sees a black panther walking stealthily along the top of his fence. The neighbour kids try to dethrone it by throwing rocks.

"Knock it off," Miles yells at the kids out the window.

The kids knock it off. The cat. The kids and cat dispersed by the time Miles stumbles downstairs and goes out to the backyard to examine his fence. Miles glances at the fence and over it, but doesn't see any damage and/or the single mother and her kids. He turns and trips over the black panther at his feet. Although this doesn't look like the same one he just saw on the fence; that one was the size of a small franchise. But who the hell knows? He's never seen such a pride of unusually large cats; he'd be hard-pressed to discern the difference between them. From his new position at ground level, he can see Mern's chrysanthemums trying to make headway amongst the weeds in the overgrown, half-dead flowerbed.

Miles gets up, tries to shoo the cat back to the pink-haired lady's yard, but the cat doesn't move. Belligerent, Miles thinks. He pushes it carefully with his bare toes. He doesn't want to provoke the cat. He wants it to go home where it belongs. The cat is crouched into the corner of the fence, and upon closer inspection, Miles realizes something is wrong with it. Its breathing is difficult. Miles picks up the cat, huge in his arms, thirty-odd pounds, possibly closer to forty, he estimates. The cat's chest labouring as if breathing water, Miles can hear the fluid in every ragged breath. The cat doesn't struggle or try to get away as Miles expects; instead the cat gives itself over and lies in Miles's arms as if he were a lifelong friend. Miles holds the cat close to his face for its last watery breaths.

Tuesday Evening:
Two bottles of rosé, two measuring cups Wild Turkey Bourbon found in the broom closet while looking for appropriate funeral shroud for panther. Also need bottle of Mr. Clean to clean up keck (his own) on kitchen floor.

Mother-in-law's voice, dial tone. Mother-in-law's voice, dial tone. Mother-in-law's voice on voice mail: "Quit Calling."

He can't pull himself together enough to go down the street and lay the deceased cat out gently on the pink-haired lady's doorstep. Instead he calls the animal shelter to come and pick up the dead panther in the Safeway shopping bag on his front step.

Day Three Wednesday:
Leftover steak and cheese potatoes, eaten cold, face down on the bed followed by a rosé is a rosé is a rosé until dawn or comatose, whichever comes first. Unmercifully, it's dawn.

Day Four Thursday:
Miles ventures down into the kitchen on the lookout for some stray bottles of wine that Mern may have stashed away. He needs another bottle of Mr. Clean. After a room-to-room search of the duplex he comes up with a few scattered bottles of wine and a half-empty two sixer of Russian cranberry vodka that someone left on purpose, though Miles can't recall them having any parties in recent years. Miles views the bottle as half-full. He finds a bottle of Windex beneath the kitchen sink to spray on the upstairs carpet that reeks of Kentucky bourbon.

Evening, Thursday:
The telephone rings rings rings just as Miles rolls over and deposits the now empty bottle of red-tinged vodka next to the bed.

"Joleanne is here with me at my mother's," Mern says. "I didn't want you to worry."

"She's pregnant." Mern pauses.

"So the mums are all accounted for?" Miles asks.

"Are you drunk?" Mern asks.

"Not so much," says Miles.

"She wants to keep the baby," Mern says. "Raymond is going to get a job—"

"Raymond? Who the hell is Raymond?"

"The hundred-pound-man is Raymond," Mern whispers into the receiver.

It's obvious that the hundred-pound-man is in the room. Miles can see all four of them sitting comfortably on his mother-in-law's pair of matching brocade sofas with the cream-coloured fringes as they speak. Miles doesn't speak.

"Joleanne wants to finish her schooling," Mern continues. "She wants to be a veterinarian."

Flash forward, Miles gets an image of his handsome grown-up daughter: her hair is permed and stylish, playful brown ringlets hang down either side of her pale face. She's holding a large sick black cat that she's diagnosed with kidney failure. "The fluid has nowhere to go and backs up into the lungs, you see," she says expertly.

"God help," Miles says in his present day

The thing about the cat that Miles can't shake despite the copious amounts of wine and cranberry vodka is how the cat laid in his arms like he were a worthy person, as if he were someone in whose arms you might choose to die in. It didn't seem to matter that he was a grade-nine drop-out or that he'd been fired from his job or had, at best, been an absent father to his 17-year-old daughter and probably a worse husband in his 15-year marriage. All that mattered to the cat at that moment was Miles's presence—something as stupid and basic as that. It's the simplicity that makes him inescapably sad.

And then he's a sobbing mess on the telephone about job loss and loss in general and Wild Turkeys and cranberry vodka and yes, he is drunk, and the produce cooler and freckled trouts, Sharoma and black panthers. He knows he's not making any sense, but he feels the need to list to Mern the events that so inelegantly played into the collapse of his coliseum.

"This I can imagine," he tells Mern. "But what I can't fathom is how far you can fall. Surely somebody should be there to pick you up?"

Although Brother Kevin, and the Mute, his counsellors-in-practice, his soul-savers, his spiritual-spin doctors, have assured him on a weekly basis that god is there, always, even if at times his silence is excruciating.

There's silence on the other end of the telephone and Miles realizes that Mern has hung up.

Another bottle of rosé, then Miles calls back five times. No one answers—not the mother-in-law, not the voice mail, not Joleanne, not Mern.

Day ???:
Heinz ketchup on loaf of stale Wonder bread. Bottle of white, two bottles of red, bottle of wine from downstairs carboy, colour indiscriminate. Bed, never left.

Saturday, perhaps:
Windex bottle empty, stench rising from carpet and bathroom alike. Attempted shower and singing, but vomited instead. Fell and hit left eye on bathroom doorknob. Shiner, like from a baseball, like Sharoma's. Last Pyrex-measured cups of random-coloured wine from basement carboy.

♟

Brother Kevin knocks tentatively at the ripped screen door. The house is dark, silent, the curtains are shut, and there is no movement. Miles peers at them from his upstairs bedroom window, doesn't move or wave. Brother Kevin waits and knocks again, a tinny knock that echoes through the empty duplex like a cheap snare drum. Brother Kevin turns and looks at his comrade. His partner-in-god shrugs. Miles sees them both look toward the young mother's house. She's outside in the backyard smoking an acrid-smelling cigarette and watering her red begonias and purple-blue irises and grapefruit-sized peonies. Her four children are running through the plastic pool.

She flicks her hand-rolled cigarette over the fence into the alley and stops to concentrate the spray from the hose on the kids for a fleeting moment. The kids whoop and holler and scream with delight, then the mother goes back to absently watering the flowers. But the kids pester her to do it again, over here mom, spray me mom, once more mom, and after a minute, the mother gives in and sits down on the back step, lights another cigarette, this one not as pungent as the first and with a bona fide filter, then she holds the hose up high and the kids revel in the sheer paradise of her watery gift, the simplicity of her mother presence.

The Mute disappears around the side of the duplex. Miles goes to the window that faces the backyard, which resembles an Arizona desert with a few patches of dried yellow grass here and there. The Mute bends down, examining perhaps, Mern's struggling chrysanthemums. There could be hope, Miles thinks, as he watches the Mute investigate the roots of a spiraea, the limp lilac bush up against the back fence. Brother Kevin joins him. The Mute goes over to the aluminum shed and digs out the sprinkler Miles didn't know they owned. Likely the same place the Jehovah's found his gas-powered lawn mower last week. Brother Kevin attaches the sprinkler to the hose lying on the ground and the Mute turns it on. The water shoots up unpredictably, too high at first, like Icarus to the dazzling sun, Miles fears. The Mute adjusts the flow, then the water catches the normal sun and reflects the colours of the spectrum, a fractured rainbow of curling, waving, erratic water. Nonetheless, a rainbow.

Too high, too fast, too soon for hope, Miles holds his head in his hands, goes back to his unmade bed. Stare out bedroom window—amazing sight: a moving, shimmering body of light and colour in motion. Sublime. Watch from the bed until darkness and falling eyelids invade.

Day Seven Sunday:
Miles plans to get out of bed. He's been lying there thinking about it for two days. His head hurts and his eyes are burning. He dreamt of vivid arcs of colour and droplets of pure light glistening and glimmering in the air, so real before his eyes they were like synchronized fireflies. Because of it, when he did manage to sleep, he imagined himself awake, and when he was awake he thought himself asleep.

Miles looks at the collection of bottles surrounding the bed: Mr. Clean, Wild Turkey, Windex, wine, Russian Vodka, Heinz ketchup—friends enough for anyone, but still, beyond his aching head, he aches. He should get up and clean up this mess in case Mern decides to come home, or Joleanne pops over to pick up some forgotten thing, (him, he hopes) but he can't seem to get out of the bed. He sees a motion out the bedroom window, a flicker of light and colour. Immediately his head starts to reel with the likelihood of delirium tremors: D.T.'s, the psychosis of chronic alcoholism complete with tremors and hallucinations. He's heard about it, but he's always prided himself on knowing when to quit, when enough was enough. He hopes this past week hasn't changed that.

He focuses on the window intently: the question of his sanity, the whole of his being, the aggregate of his future life, whether he ends up alone or reunited with his wife and daughter, rides on these next few seconds. His eyes are burning. His head feels like Swiss cheese, his stomach roiling and empty; his soul needs sustenance. He sits up shakily on the edge of the bed staring closely out the bedroom window—and There!

He sees it again, a gesturing arm of colour followed by its absence, then the colour accompanied by the iridescent light—it can't possibly be real. As he watches, it comes again and again crossing back and forth over his window, cyclic, like droughts, Miles thinks, like seasons, like rainy days to plan for.

Miles pulls himself up and walks over to the bedroom window. He sees the single mother in the next yard playing duck, duck, goose with the daycare kids and her own, too, something he's never witnessed before. In his own backyard he sees the sprinkler he neglected to turn off yesterday. If he squints hard enough he can see the grass starting to green up amongst the weeds.

He watches the sprinkler go back and forth for several moments, and then goes downstairs. The silence in the duplex is deafening. He doesn't turn on the rosewood altar of his monstrous television. Instead he sits quietly at the kitchen table holding his sobriety for as long as he can, gazing out the kitchen window at the sparkling, falling droplets of water. And if god doesn't happen to come-a-calling that day, then he might have to go out and look for the two of them.

## The Nothing Yard

My father drives past the General Store, which triples as the Post Office, The One-hour Martinizer and the Sears Catalogue Outlet. We pass by Our Lady of Lourdes church that stands tall and white and pure, seemingly untouchable with wheat flowing on all sides of it like ochre water. It's the last thing you see down the earth road to Tall Hank's and Marge's.

My father wheels our sedan into the yard. The nothing yard, I call it because there's no barn, no fence, no barking-bounding dog or cat whose fur should smell of fresh manure. Not even that. Not even the boy. Only a solitary horse, bony and drab red standing next to the coral faded house.

Tall Hank comes out of nowhere, in long, wide strides wiping his hands on a crimson rag. The red horse starts to follow but Hank says something and she retreats back to the shade of the house. I watch behind for the brown-faced boy but he doesn't come. We run to Tall Hank. My brothers attach themselves to his knees and hard thighs. Hank laughs loud and funny with his sparrow-brown eyes and hollow cheeks that would look awfully dismal if he wasn't smiling.

Marge appears in the doorway, waves her tiny hands and smiles, red-faced and warm. Hank rises with my brothers attached, my sister in one arm, and the other he drapes across my shoulders. Together we climb the wood steps like an insect ascending treacherous terrain.

## The Nothing Yard

When we reach Marge, then I forget about the brown-faced boy. I remember instead what I like about Marge is that she doesn't tower over me like everyone else. In fact that year, I am taller.

My father goes over and smoothes his hand along the barrel of the horse's body like he's trying to soften the harsh lines of her protruding ribs while my mother sorts through our leftover lunch on the hood of our black sedan.

"She's down a few pounds here, Hank," my father hollers. "Whaddya feeding her—celery sticks?"

My mother, who is no stranger to diets, winks up at Marge. Marge waits and they go into the house together. Hank stands on the porch scowling while my father feeds leftover corn chips from his flat palm to the horse.

Inside the house, Marge shoos us into the living room. My father slides into a rocking chair and lights a cigar. The dark odour of his cigar smoke smells like a smouldering blanket and seeps silently into the folds of Marge's white sheers. I listen carefully as Tall Hank tells our father about how the year before last the grasshoppers came.

"They came like a black cloud, chirping and buzzing and clicking in the sky. Then they landed, all at once—you never seen anything like it, Semi. They covered half a section."

My father raises a brow at this. I thought maybe that was why the yard was like that and ask Hank if this is so.

Tall Hank rocks back and forth, slaps both hands on his dusty trousers. His cheeks are hollow and he laughs until tears come to his eyes. I watch him from the sofa and laugh, too, although I don't know why.

Then the laughter stops but the tears don't. Hank covers his face in his hands. My father watches helplessly until my mother comes in and puts her arm around Hank. That makes Hank cry even more. Marge comes over to the sofa and hugs me. Tears threaten my eyes, too and Marge hugs me harder. Hank raises his face from his hands and sees me clinging onto Marge's shoulders that scarcely support her own tiny frame but now support a gangly adolescent boy. Hank erupts, sudden and reckless. His eyes glitter and for a moment there's no sound except for Hank's unexpected laughter.

With a sweep of his arms Hank herds us into the kitchen. Marge sets a basket of steaming donuts on the table. She talks and gestures with both hands in the air about the grasshoppers, filling the space of a minute ago like it never happened. After five donuts apiece, my brothers and I get up to go outside. Hank gets up also and tries to wipe the icing sugar from our faces. My brothers stand obediently. I swerve around the kitchen.

"I'm twelve," I tell him but still he tries, then finally he laughs and gives up. He picks up my brothers and carries them down the steep stairs. He sets them free and they take off charging through the belly-high wheat in search of gophers. It's hot and I go over and lie on the hood of our sedan. It's harvest time, yet no one works in the field.

The horse ambles over and nuzzles her velvet mouth in my shirt. Hank comes and grabs her roughly by the mane. He raises his arms and yells, "Ya, Ya!" The horse bolts for the field and does not turn to look back until she's but a colourless speck in the distance.

♟

The next morning as the sun makes an appearance on the flat horizon, my mother rearranges her hair in the spare bedroom. I check out the 4-H ribbons and medals that hang on the wall.

## The Nothing Yard

Black and white photographs are stuck haphazardly around the frame of the mirror in which my mother is tucking and spraying her auburn bouffant.

"That's Hank as a youngster," my mother says. He's standing full up in the stirrups on a horse that is clearly not the one outside. No, this horse looks potent and intense. Its dun coat shimmers in the sunshine.

My father is already downstairs. He's dressed in his black suit that he wears only for the most earnest of occasions. Hank stands at the stove in a stiff white shirt and black bow tie flipping saskatoon berry pancakes on a griddle. He smells like pinecones. Marge has a smooth black dress on. We wait for our mother to come downstairs. That's when I spot the small, blurry photograph on the windowsill. I have to squint to see through the fogged glass to see Tall Hank and Marge. The brown-faced boy is perched bareback on a horse. Hank's hand rests on the boy's leg. He looks to be around my age. The three of them stand side-by-side in the yard with nothing around them except for wheat and dust. And even though it's hard to tell, I know Hank is smiling because his cheeks are hollow.

My mother comes down the stairs. I stop looking at the picture to look at her. Her dress is black like Marge's. Her bouffant is perfect, her lips a cardinal red. She smiles at my father who stops reading the newspaper to look at her, also. I feel flowers in the air as she passes by.

Hank takes the pancakes off the griddle and flips them affably in the air, then unto my plate. I eat pancake after pancake that my father says are going to bust my guts if I don't stop. Little Marge laughs. I gaze across the table at her, smiling like she did in the picture. And then I remember to ask about the brown-faced boy.

The whole kitchen goes quiet save for the Pyrex coffee pot murmuring soft liquid sighs on the stovetop. Marge looks frightened, so does my mother. Hank examines the cloudy glass with the tips of his fingers, and then he lays the picture down.

No one says anything as Hank goes out the door. My father rises but Marge lifts her head from her arms and says, "Leave him be." She gets up and goes upstairs.

My mother clears the dishes from the table as if she's in a hurry. My father helps, too, which is something he never does at home. The two of them stand at the sink talking in hushed voices. My mother looks to see if we are listening.

"Why don't you go outside and find Hank?" she says to me as she wipes saskatoon berries from my sister's copper curls. She releases her into the living room to watch cartoons with my brothers.

I know then, though no one has come out and said it, that it isn't because of the grasshoppers that came, or about the belly-high section of wheat that is full and ripe and ready to harvest, but no one is going to do it this year. I know then it's about the brown-faced boy, who isn't there in the nothing yard. And the horse outside that is wasting away, the same way the boy must have from *cancer*, I overheard my mother hiss to my father.

I stand outside in the yard. Early morning dew still rests on the few violas that manage, miraculously, year after year, to carry on in this unforgiving land. I don't want to go find Hank. I don't even see him amongst the wheat until I look around for the horse. She's in the field with Hank. That's when I see the shotgun. I run across the yard and bound up the steps.

"Dad?"

My father is finished drying the dishes and sits at the table smoking yesterday's cigar. My mother is exhaling cigarette smoke out the screened window. My father looks at me, but it's as if he doesn't see me.

"Dad?"

My mother gasps from the window.

"Oh, my Christ, Semi, he's got a gun. Hank's got a gun!"

My father bolts outside and runs towards the field while my mother and I watch from the window. My father stops at the perimeter of the field like there is an invisible barrier. The horse wanders around Hank in close range. Hank remains motionless with the gun at his side.

My mother and I stare out the window, transfixed by this figment of Hank, who not ten minutes ago was standing in this kitchen flipping pancakes in the air. Now he stands in the field looking like a menace with a shotgun in his right hand. The horse tries to nuzzle him. Hank yells but the horse doesn't bolt, only shies away slightly, and stays close—almost as if she knows. She is so close to Hank that he has no chance to raise the gun. The horse shadows his body. Hank doesn't turn. My father stands in the yard.

Without warning the horse nudges Hank roughly. Hank is momentarily knocked off-balance. When he regains himself, Hank whirls, raises his shotgun and points it at the horse. The horse does not flinch nor does she make a move to run. Instead she offers her left side to Hank as if she's waiting for him to mount up and ride her bareback like he did so many times before with the boy. Or shoot her.

Hank presses the barrel of the shotgun into the barrel of the horse.

"Oh, my god, he's going to gut-shoot her," my mother exhales her cigarette smoke.

"What's gut-shoot?" I ask.

My mother pushes me away.

Outside in the morning stillness, I hear the click of the safety releasing. My father wades into the wheat. I resume my place next to my mother who doesn't seem to notice I'm there.

The horse does the strangest thing. She starts to circle Hank—the two of them connected by the barrel of the gun. She moves slowly as if tethered and Hank spins with her like a spoke in a wheel. My father stops and stands thirty feet out from Hank, afraid, perhaps to go any closer. Maybe he's seen it before, people so swollen with grief, you don't know what they'll do. The whole scene is absurd, like some bizarre, practiced ritual of rider and horse, except this one includes a fully-loaded shotgun.

Marge appears and marches across the field. She strides out past my father. She has something in her hand. What Marge is going to do, none of us can guess. Nor can we guess what Hank will do, either. All we know is that horse and man are connected by something other than the gun pressed into the horse's jutting ribs.

And maybe Marge knows this, too, and is calling Hank's bluff, or debunking some arcane code of death, or whatever eerie thing takes over us all when someone close dies. Marge reaches Hank as the horse passes in front. Hank pivots with the horse and does not allow the gun to drop. When Marge catches a glimpse of Hank's face, his cheeks are tear-stained; his mouth works mutely. Hank and the horse continue like a merry-go-round. Neither one wants to go on. Neither one can stop.

Then Marge steps into the arena of Hank and horse. When the gun reaches her, the pair stops. Marge extends her hand, gives something to Hank.

"It's time to go to the funeral," she says. Hank glances at the arcing sun, at Our Lady of Lourdes on the horizon standing alone, nothing but wood and faith. Marge leaves Hank with his shotgun cocked and pressed into the body of the horse. She makes my father leave also. He keeps glancing back as if he's not sure whether Hank will shoot the horse or himself or both. When they reach the house, Marge sits at the kitchen table in her black dress like she's waiting for something—the *whump* of a shotgun, perhaps.

After a while the whump doesn't come but Hank does. He appears in the doorway looking hailed out. Marge waits while Hank splashes water on his face, and after last minute instructions to me, my parents and Hank and Marge climb into our sedan and depart.

Hours later the sun has grown dim, lost its heat. I hear heavy footsteps on the porch stairs. Marge's eyes are the colour of my mother's faded lipstick and Hank's cheeks look as if they might sink into his face and disappear forever. I am glad they are home.

⚑

The next morning, packed and ready to go, Hank crouches down and hugs me fiercely. Marge and my mother laugh and cry at the same time. Hank goes over and Marge cries into his belly.

What Marge gave Hank—I don't know. I still don't know. Maybe she gave him a 4-H ribbon or a medal from the spare bedroom or that photograph of the three of them. Perhaps she gave him memory. There are times in this life when memories are all we have. Memories of a boy's laughter on the wind, someone to make donuts for or wipe crumbs from small faces—the sweet, immeasurable weight of a child's embrace.

Who knows? But whatever she gave Hank, she gave herself, too.

The last thing I see is Hank and Marge standing side-by-side in the yard with nothing around them except for wheat and dust. And even though it's hard to tell because the dust gets in the way, I can see Hank's cheeks, hollow and smiling.